CARING FOR HIS CHILD

BY
AMY ANDREWS

MILLS & BOON®

First published in Great Britain 2006
Large Print edition 2007
Harlequin Mills & Boon Limited,
Eton House, 18-24 Paradise Road,
Richmond, Surrey TW9 1SR

© Amy Andrews 2006

ISBN-13: 978 0 263 19339 8
ISBN-10:   0 263 19339 X

Set in Times Roman 17 on 20½ pt.
17-0307-49482

Printed and bound in Great Britain
by Antony Rowe Ltd, Chippenham, Wiltshire

'Thank you for keeping me updated on Miranda's condition,' she said stiffly.

'You didn't return my calls.' David sat at the breakfast bar and watched her.

Fran stirred her tea, not missing the gentle tone of accusation in his voice. She tapped the teaspoon on the side of the mug and placed it in the sink. 'I'm leaving, David. What would have been the point? Better to make a clean break.'

'So, you're running away?'

'Yes,' she admitted quietly.

'Why? I know you love me, Fran. Love us. It doesn't make any sense.'

Her eyes welled with tears and she felt a sob rise in her throat. 'Because if I love you this much now, how bad is it going to be in a year, or two, or five?' She knew her voice was rising and that soon she wouldn't be able to speak. 'What if I can't do it then? What if I'm useless to you?' She sat at the table with him and put a hand on his arm. 'It's better to get out now, while I still have a chance to recover.'

'It doesn't matter where you run, Fran, It's too late. We're in your heart, in your soul. You can run, but we'll always be with you.'

As a twelve-year-old, **Amy Andrews** used to sneak off with her mother's romance novels and devour every page. She was the type of kid who daydreamed a lot and carried a cast of thousands around in her head, and from quite an early age knew that it was her destiny to write. So, in between her duties as wife and mother, her paid job as a Paediatric Intensive Care Nurse and her compulsive habit to volunteer, she did just that! Amy Andrews lives in Brisbane's beautiful Samford Valley, with her very wonderful and patient husband, two gorgeous kids, a couple of black Labradors and six chooks.

Recent titles by the same author:

CARING FOR HIS CHILD

This book is dedicated to all those
people who have made the ultimate
selfless decision at the most tragic time in
their lives. Your precious gift gives others
another chance at life. Remember—
don't take your organs to heaven.
Heaven knows we need them here.

CHAPTER ONE

FRAN PUSHED OPEN the wooden shutters and inhaled the salty sea air. For the first time in two years a feeling of contentment surfaced. The silent grey ocean was a good match for the dark storm clouds on a chilly winter's afternoon, but despite the inclement weather the beach beckoned.

She heard the clatter of paws on the highly polished wooden floor behind her and turned to see Fonzie, her black Labrador puppy, sliding to a halt at her feet. His ridiculously big paws made him awkward and clumsy and Fran swore he grinned at her as he sat looking up at her expectantly.

She knelt and gave him a scratch behind the ears and he gave her a I'll-be-your-slave-for-life look. 'Come on, boy, let's go for a walk on the beach.'

He licked her face and Fran laughed. It echoed in the empty house and she couldn't wait for the morning when the van would arrive with all her worldly goods and she could fill up the dinky little renovated beachfront cottage she'd been inexplicably drawn to two months ago.

She grabbed his lead and pulled on her hooded jumper as she walked out the door. She clipped the lead to Fonzie's collar and opened the white picket gate, crossed the narrow laneway and traversed the small area of grass with the little black puppy eagerly pulling against his restraint all the way.

They reached the concrete stairs that led down to the beach and the dog stopped abruptly. He looked up at her soulfully and she chuckled as she gave in and picked him up, carrying him down the dozen steps. At only ten weeks old she supposed the stairs could have seemed daunting.

But once her foot hit the sand, Fonzie squirmed to be put down and pulled excitedly at the lead, charging up and down the beach of the small cove several times with Fran in tow, before he was content to sit at the water's edge and chase the waves.

Fran sat farther back where the sand was drier and watched as Fonzie followed the ebb and flow of the tide. She had her legs hugged against her body and her head resting on her knees. A light wind blew up and lifted a few strands of her long blond hair across her face.

She tucked them behind her ear and laughed as a solitary seagull landing nearby glared haughtily at an excited Fonzie. They had a brief stand-off, with Fonzie backing down as the bird ran towards him, wings expanded menacingly. She'd laughed more in the last couple of weeks, having Fonzie around, than she had in the last couple of years. Buying the dog had definitely been a good move.

Fran tuned in to the sound of the gentle lapping of the waves as they kissed the sand and felt each one soothing the ache that had taken up permanent residence in her heart. *It will be*

OK. It will be OK. It will be OK. The words
echoed with every roll of surf against sand and
Fran knew she had come to the right place to
recover and regain her life.

'Oh, look, Daddy, it's a puppy. Isn't he
so-o-o-o cute?'

Fran had been so deep in thought she hadn't
seen or heard the approach of other visitors to
the beach. She startled as the high voice of a
young girl broke into her reverie.

'Can I, please, pat your puppy?'

Fran looked at the child and felt the familiar
rush of painful emotions swamp her like a tidal
wave. The girl had skinny arms and legs and
her curly red hair sprang out in riotous disorder
all over her head. Her cute moon-shaped face
was smattered with freckles and her eyes were
a deep sea green. She looked about twelve, the
same age Daisy would have been, and every
cell in Fran's body ordered her to retreat.

No, she wanted to say. You can't pat Fonzie.
Go away. I don't want to see you and I don't
want to talk to you. I don't want to share this

beach with you. Can't you see I just want to be left alone?

Then the girl, who was waiting patiently for Fran's permission, snaked a finger into her curls and proceeded to absently twirl a strand of hair. And Fran felt like she'd been stabbed through the heart with a machete.

Daisy had done that. Exactly that. From the time she had been able to co-ordinate baby brain and fingers to do it, she had done it. She'd done it when she'd been sleepy or concentrating or bored or watching television or cuddling up. Some children sucked their thumbs. Some carried around bits of material that had seen better days. Daisy had twirled her hair.

As she silently inspected the child before her, Fran had to admit there wasn't one other thing about the girl that reminded her of her daughter. Physically, the resemblance was non-existent. In fact, Daisy had been the complete opposite in looks, taking very much after Fran and her Nordic ancestry. Tall and blond. Fair complexion, light blue eyes.

But that gesture, that hair twirl was Daisy personified and Fran despaired at how much it still hurt to catch a glimpse of her daughter. When would an incident like this be comforting and joyful, as she had been assured would one day happen? When would she be able to see her daughter in someone else's child and be grateful and at peace? When would the hurt ever stop?

'I'm terribly sorry.' A male voice intruded into her pain. 'Mirry, sweetie, I think the lady would like to be left alone.'

David Ross watched the woman as she turned her head to face him. The pain in her eyes took his breath away. The sadness. The grief. Yes, this was definitely a woman who wanted to be left alone. Then she blinked and straightened and it was as if she'd drawn the curtain on her emotions. A wary veneer was all that remained.

Fran looked at Mirry and forced a smile onto her dry lips. 'Of course you can pat Fonzie. I'm sure he'd love it.'

Mirry jiggled with delight and ran down to the shoreline. Fran and David watched them for a few moments.

He made a mental note to make sure Mirry washed her hands when they got back home. 'She's never going to let up about a dog now.' He grinned.

Fran looked at him, startled by his voice again, and gave him a ghost of a smile. She looked back at Fonzie and his new friend and wondered if it would be rude to leave.

'I'm David Ross,' he said, and Fran turned in time to see him put his hand out to be shaken.

'Fran,' she said quietly, and slid her hand briefly into his. It was warm and she suddenly realised how cold hers was. How cold she was all over. She hugged her legs closer.

'Are you just passing through Ashworth Bay?'

Go away. Don't talk to me. But she couldn't say it. Even with everything that had happened over the last two years, she still felt an entrenched politeness, a societal expectation that wouldn't allow her to be just plain rude.

Although she was tempted. After all, how bad could his reaction be?

Would it make her feel worse than the day they'd switched her daughter's life support off? Or her marriage falling apart? If you could make it through those things then nothing that anyone thought about you mattered a damn.

'No. I've just bought a cottage on the cliff.'

David felt a flutter of excitement. 'Really? You must be our new neighbour. We weren't expecting you till tomorrow. Mirry will be very excited. Hey, maybe I won't have to get her that puppy after all. She can puppy-sit for you.'

She looked at him silently and battled the urge to bellow in utter despair. She didn't want to live next door to this man and his daughter. She didn't want to know them. She didn't want to have nice neighbourly chats. And she didn't need a puppy-sitter.

Sure, he seemed nice enough. He was tall and had a friendly face and intelligent eyes, blue like hers but darker, richer, deeper. Like a sapphire. He was lean rather than bulky and she noticed how he had long elegant-looking fingers, as if he spent all day playing piano concertos. No doubt he'd make a great neighbour, but that wasn't why she'd come to Ashworth Bay.

David waited for an answer but could tell he wasn't going to get one. His new neighbour obviously liked to play things close to her chest. She looked like she'd rather be anywhere but right there, talking to him…or not, as was the case.

'Fonzie,' Fran called, brushing off her hands and rising to her feet. 'Come on, boy, time to go home.'

The black ball of fur hurtled towards her and wagged his tail vigorously as he stood at her feet. Mirry followed closely. She fell onto her knees beside Fonzie and averted her face to protect it from the puppy's appreciative licks.

'Miranda, sweetie, this is Fran. Or would you prefer Mrs…?' David asked.

'Fran is fine,' she said, stiff-lipped.

'Fran is our new neighbour,' David informed his daughter.

'Really?' Miranda's excitement was barely contained, her voice almost a squeal. 'Can I come and visit Fonzie later?'

David laughed at his daughter's eagerness and lack of pretence. Maybe he should have been cross but it was such a pleasure to see. His daughter didn't trust easily. Years of doctors and hospitals and painful treatments had seen to that. But she'd certainly taken an instant liking to Fran and Fonzie.

He watched Fran distance herself even more, her eyes going from light blue to glacial blue in an instant. Man, she had baggage! She looked like she'd splinter into a thousand pieces if he or Mirry managed to break through the force-field she had erected. And he should know, it had taken him way too long to break through his own.

Which was a real shame because she was stunningly beautiful…or at least she could have been. She was tall with gorgeous platinum-blond hair, straight as an arrow and falling almost to her waist. But the ends were split hinting that its length was due more to it being neglected rather than any fashion statement.

Her cheekbones were high, if a little too prominent, her milky complexion wan and pale, rather than healthy and luminous. Her face was completely devoid of make-up, as if she didn't care that her features were too angular where once they'd probably been regal. Her face hinted at the gauntness reflected in the rest of her body.

Faded denim hung loosely around legs that had probably filled the jeans perfectly once upon a time. As she bent to Fonzie he noticed how the waist of her jeans had slipped lower, barely clinging to the jut of angular hips. Her baggy jumper was unable to disguise the scrawniness of her chest, the flatness of her breasts or the boniness of her shoulders.

Fran was a woman who hadn't been taking care of herself and, unfortunately, that was also something he understood too well. How grief could be so overwhelming that eating, sleeping, grooming didn't register as important. How only breathing…existing, putting one foot in front of the other, living from one second to the next was all you could manage.

'I think we need to let Fran get settled first,' David said to his daughter.

Fran stared at them both for a moment longer, more grateful to David than he would ever know at the reprieve he had afforded her. She gave them a small smile and turned away, dragging a reluctant Fonzie up the beach back to the house. She kept her eyes on the row of cottages set back a little from the face of the cliff and failed to feel her earlier contentment. A girl called Miranda had snatched it away and the wind had blown it out of reach.

'She seems sad, Daddy,' Miranda said as she and David watched the forlorn figure walk away, her baggy jeans threatening to slide off her hips with each footfall.

David nodded, not surprised at the astuteness of his twelve-year-old daughter. Miranda had seen a lot of sadness and had always been sensitive to people's emotions.

'Yes, honey,' he agreed, 'she does.'

'Never mind.' Miranda grinned up at her father. 'We can cheer her up, can't we?'

David doubted it somehow but he didn't want to quash Miranda's spirit. If anyone could do it, she could. 'I'm sure we can, sweetie, I'm sure we can.'

Fran reached the solace of her new home gratefully. She felt chilled to the bone. Yes, it had been cold on the beach but she knew it wasn't just that. How was she going to cope with having a twelve-year-old girl as a neighbour? A constant reminder of what she'd lost?

Her heart, her emotions had frosted over at the mere thought. She had felt the chill invading her skin, creeping into her bones steadily each second she had spent in their company on the beach. And despite their distance now, she couldn't shake it. Had fate not already dealt her more than one person could deal with?

She rubbed her arms vigorously, the cold penetrating deeply, diffusing its icy breath into every cell and fibre of her body. She was not emotionally ready for Miranda. Existing had been the only thing she'd been capable of these last two years. She'd come here to live again, start over, but she needed to do that on her own terms and in her own time.

Maybe Miranda didn't live with David full time? Maybe she was the product of a broken home and she only spent a few days a fortnight with her father. The thought cheered Fran even as it appalled her. How could she wish that on someone as sweet as Mirry?

She plonked herself down on the old-fashioned padded seat that had been built into the bay window and stared unseeingly as night advanced over the ocean and across the beach. Fonzie joined her and dozed on her feet, exhausted from his earlier exercise, a warm fuzzy blanket. She was too cold and numb to move, paralysed by a resurfacing of emotion that she hadn't been prepared for.

She had been so sure when she'd seen the cottage for sale on-line that it was her destiny to live here. It had appealed to something deep inside. Had it been the lure of fulfilling a life-long fantasy of living in a house by the sea or some kind of instinct? Whatever…her gut had said yes even though, at that stage, she hadn't yet decided to move.

Maybe before she'd decided to travel one and a half thousand kilometres away from her home town of Canberra and all her family and friends, she should have sussed out the neighbours a bit better? But the real estate agent had assured her that Ashworth Bay was populated mainly by retirees and a sleepy seaside town full of oldies had sounded ideal.

Her view across the bay was uninterrupted and she could see the Ashworth Bay Nursing Home standing in all its pre-war grandeur on the cliffs opposite, its white-columned façade an imposing site for any passing maritime traffic. Once a grand hotel when Ashworth Bay had been in its heyday, it still held a commanding presence.

And hopefully, tomorrow, she would be working there. She rubbed her arms again and pushed the nervous flutter aside when she thought about the fact that she hadn't nursed in two years. Part of her plan to get her life back together involved going back to work, and she would not deviate from it.

For goodness' sake, it was a small nursing home in a sleepy seaside town—how hard could it be? She'd worked in a busy city emergency department for years. An old folk's home should be a doddle compared to that.

Finally, it started to penetrate her brain cells that her core temperature was getting a little too low to support basic body functions and she stirred herself. Fonzie briefly opened one eye at her movement but preferred his repose and promptly shut it again.

She pulled out a change of clothes from her suitcase and padded through the empty house to the bathroom. All the utilities were in working order and Fran stood under the hot shower for a long time, waiting for sensation to return to her numb extremities. She wished it was as easy to melt the coldness around her heart, to relieve the ache, obliterate the pain but she knew only time could mend those wounds. And just as well she wasn't holding her breath.

She dressed warmly in a tracksuit and roused a sleeping Fonzie, driving down to the main street and pulling up out the front of the fish-and-chip shop, more for something to do than for any nutritional reason. The crumbed fish and hot chips looked great and smelt fantastic, but as usual Fran struggled to be interested.

Her appetite was appalling. She ate because she knew that her body had to fulfil certain biological functions to keep going and for that it needed fuel—but that was it. Fran had totally lost her love of food. The pure and utter joy that eating something wonderful gave your soul. The aromas, the tastes, the textures. Eating had become purely functional.

She had lost weight. Too much weight. But try as she may she was only capable of nibbling. Looking at the generous portion in front of her, she knew that Fonzie was about to score well. The mere thought of such a large helping was nauseating.

She munched on a chip and looked up towards the now subtly lit façade of the nursing home and quashed a nervous pang, thinking about her two o'clock interview the next day. OK, so she hadn't worked since Daisy had died but she'd come to Ashworth Bay to start afresh and get her life back on track. And that included a job.

Receiving her decree nisi had been just the right impetus for her to realise that her life was a shambles. Appalled by her lack of emotion towards a piece of paper that should have been devastating, she'd known she had to do something with her life or she was going to slowly wither and die.

Fonzie licked her leg and Fran dragged her attention back to him. He had such a forlorn look on his face. The smell of her food had obviously been appreciated much more by him and he gave her a little puppy bark as much as to say, Hey, what about me?

Fran scratched him behind the ears and

placed the paper on the ground with most of the food untouched. A few chips and two mouthfuls of the fish had been all she'd been able to stomach. Fonzie, on the other hand, ate heartily, not stopping until every last morsel had been licked from the paper.

She gathered her stuff and drove home, Fonzie leaping out of the car as she opened the door. She gave chase and he looked back over his shoulder and barked excitedly at this great game they were playing. He ran into the neighbour's yard through their open gate and Fran couldn't believe it when the black ball of fur barrelled straight through the cat flap in the front door.

Great. What would be the chances that this was an elderly spinster's house and not Miranda's? The door opened and Fran saw Miranda, giggling as she accepted happy licks from the traitorous puppy. David was laughing, too.

'I'm so sorry,' Fran said, retrieving her dog from Miranda. 'He was too quick for me. I hope he didn't upset your cat.'

'No fear of that,' said David, stroking Fonzie's back. 'The cat is no more.'

David looked awkward and Fran guessed there was some story behind the cat.

The child gave Fonzie a big squeeze with her skinny arms and reluctantly handed him back. 'He can come and visit any time, can't he, Daddy?' said Miranda.

'Sure,' said David, reaching out to pat Fonzie and noting Fran's slight movement backwards. She looked like she'd rather saw off her arm than stay.

Fran smiled politely and started to back away.

'Are you staying the night?' asked David.

Fran froze and so did any sort of coherent thought. 'Ah…yes.'

He laughed and it was such a lovely deep rich sound that Fran gave a surprised blink.

'Did you sneak your furniture in when I wasn't looking?'

'I'll be OK for tonight. I have a few things and Fonzie…'

'Well, if you need anything, just yell.'

Fran looked at Miranda, her head resting against her father's waist, a finger twirling a lock of hair, and thought, Never going to happen.

CHAPTER TWO

FRAN LAY AWAKE most of the night. So much for contentment and finding a place to heal. Meeting Miranda had been like twisting the knife that had been thrust into her heart two years ago. Of course it wasn't possible to go through life and never have to deal with children, but did she have to live next door to one?

So much for the calming effects of waves! The therapeutic white noise of sea against sand! Every time Fran shut her eyes she could see Mirry twisting her hair around her finger and sweet, sweet Daisy's laughter would tinkle through her head. Every cell in her body mourned the loss of her beautiful daughter.

Fran hugged herself to stop the ache in her arms. The ache that could only be assuaged by the feel and weight of Daisy's body as she snuggled up close and said, 'I love you, Mummy.'

She dozed off around dawn, frantic that if she didn't get some sleep she was going to look as old and haggard as she felt these days, and the director of nursing would want to admit her as a patient instead of employing her. There was so much to do today, she needed to be on the ball.

Fonzie licked her forehead a couple of hours later and she opened her eyes as his sweet puppy breath warmed her face.

'OK, boy,' she said. Time to let him out. He'd been so good with his house-training. She got out of her bed reluctantly into the chilly morning air and dressed in her tracksuit from the night before. She could hear the waves calling and decided a walk on the beach would do them both good.

Some cold sea air would hopefully blast the fuzzy cotton-wool feeling from her brain and invigorate her body for the day ahead. Fonzie stood at the front door, wagging his tail, eagerly waiting for his mistress to get her act together. He barked impatiently and Fran acknowledged it'd be just as good for him—give him a much-needed outlet for all his crazy puppy energy.

David was standing at his bay window when Fran and Fonzie passed by. He watched her as she walked down to the beach and smiled as the small puppy dragged her up and down the beach repeatedly. Even at this distance her body language gave away her profound grief.

Her shoulders were hunched, her head bowed, her steps shuffling. She was totally missing the beauty that surrounded her as she stared fixedly at the sand. The sun sparkled on the calm blue ocean like a generous god had thrown armfuls of diamonds into the sea and the cloudless blue sky arced perfectly down to the horizon as if drawn by someone who not only appreciated beauty but symmetry.

What was Fran's story? Something had caused her immense grief. Recently, too, unless her trauma was so deep, so awful, she'd been unable to move through the grief process. She was here alone. A messy break-up? A death? Who—a lover, a parent, a sibling?

'Oh, look, Daddy, it's Fran and Fonzie.' Miranda pointed. 'Can I play with him when they come back?'

David couldn't explain it but, watching the hunched figure on the beach, he suddenly felt as if he knew Fran. He didn't know her story but he knew her pain and every fibre of his being was urging him to not give up on her but to persist. To be patient and kind and help her see that there was a light at the end of the tunnel.

He knew that better than anybody. He was a perfect living example of the sentiment 'This, too, will pass'. He sighed. Helping Fran wasn't going to be easy but in a strange kind of way it almost felt like his destiny.

David smiled down at his daughter and shook his head. For some reason he couldn't articulate, he was reluctant to let Mirry unleash herself on Fran. He had noticed his new neighbour's reaction to his daughter yesterday and Fran definitely didn't want to get involved.

Although maybe a grab-life-by-the-tail-and-swing-around-wildly type of twelve-year-old girl was just what Fran needed. Maybe she needed someone just like Miranda to get through whatever it was, as much as he had needed her to get through his stuff.

'You have to get to school, madam, and I have to go to work.' He tapped her freckled nose. 'Have you taken your meds?'

'Yes, Daddy,' she said, rolling her eyes at him. 'You ask me that every morning.'

'That's because I love you and they're—'

'Important. I know.'

She gave her father a cheeky grin and ran off to get dressed for school. David felt his heart contract as it spilled over with love for his precious daughter. He turned back to the solitary figure on the beach, feeling a strange affinity for the mysterious Fran.

David knew what it felt like to be swamped with a grief that was so black and dark you couldn't fight your way through it. Didn't even want to try. Couldn't care whether you lived or died. In fact, dying was an attractive alternative. To be at peace, to not have to bear the pain any more….

Fran made herself a cup of tea from the limited supplies she had brought with her yesterday and sat at the bay window. She pulled her legs up and cradled the mug between her hands and her knees, grateful for the warmth seeping into her numb fingers.

The beach had certainly blasted out the cobwebs but it didn't take long on a winter's morning to feel chilled to the bone. She blew absently at the hot brew and was grateful to Fonzie when he leapt up to join her, plonking himself over her feet.

She stared at the nursing home on the cliff opposite and wondered what it would be like to work there. She'd never really had any geriatric experience and she hoped it wouldn't go against her. Oh, she'd done the regulation amount during her training but it hadn't been her cup of tea. The faster-paced, more exciting specialties had been more her forte.

Still, even if it was boring, it was work. Five days a week where she could take a break from her own problems, get her mind off her life and the things that had happened. Staying at home and moping may have been all she'd been capable of for a long time, but it hadn't done her any good. If she wanted to recover then she had to get back into life. And people worked.

Her stomach growled at her but she knew she couldn't face anything. She got up and made herself another cup of tea instead, sitting back in the bay window. The sun streamed through the glass and gradually warmed her up, and she felt herself drifting off to sleep.

A loud blaring of a truck's horn woke her about fifteen minutes later and she was grateful that she'd finished her tea or she would have been wearing it. She checked her watch—eight o'clock already!

The rest of the morning passed in a daze of furniture and boxes and directing big strong strapping men. She worked solidly for hours, grabbing a few cups of tea along the way because she was too busy to stop. And, anyway, the cupboards were bare. She would have to do some grocery shopping after her interview.

Fonzie thought the whole exercise was a great lark. The movers had indulged him and he had run around happily, playing with all the packing paper and exploring empty boxes. Fran hoped he would be OK at the cottage without her for the couple of hours she would be away. The yard was fully fenced and he'd no doubt have a ball. But what if he fretted? What if he barked and upset the neighbourhood because he missed her? She'd only had him for a few weeks but the thought of him being lonely and sad was unbearable.

Fran fussed about what to wear. Nothing in her wardrobe fit her anymore and she really hadn't been in the mood for shopping for a long time. Ordinarily these days what she put on didn't even register—she just grabbed whatever came to hand. But this was an interview. She may have been out of touch with the world but she was sure you still had to make a good impression.

She decided on a pair of navy dress trousers, a turtle-necked white top and a matching blue jacket. They hung on her a bit but the jacket mostly concealed that fact. She tied her hair back into a plait to hide its could-really-do-with-a-wash status. She'd run out of time this morning and anyway…it'd only been a few days.

Looking at herself critically in the bathroom mirror, Fran knew she should put on some make-up to add a bit of colour to her pale face. But she'd got out of the habit and doubted whether it would disguise much anyway. It'd probably just emphasise the things she was trying to hide.

It shouldn't matter what she looked like anyway. She wasn't going for a photo shoot or a job as a supermodel. How she looked and whether she wore make-up or not should be completely immaterial. She applied a quick coat of gloss to conceal the dryness of her lips but left it at that.

Fran took the five-minute drive around the headland and pulled up in the car park of the Ashworth Bay Nursing Home with a few minutes to spare. As she climbed out of the car she felt light-headedness wash over her and she gripped the car door for a few seconds until it passed. Come on, Franny, pull yourself together. Don't let nerves stuff this up!

The extensive grounds and magnificent gardens were hard to ignore as she walked on shaky legs up the path that led to the front door. Rose bushes lined either side.

A little old lady came rushing out the door towards her, handbag in tow, surprisingly spritely for someone who looked to be in her eighties at least. Her deeply lined face was creased with concern and her thinning white hair looked wild against her worried face.

'Oh, my dear, can you help me?' the woman asked, reaching out to Fran with a wrinkled hand. Her voice had an audible quaver and it was clear that the woman was extremely agitated about something as Fran clasped the old lady's hand.

'Goodness, my dear,' she said, looking at Fran with keen insight, 'you look terrible and have the coldest hands. You need to get in by the fire. Pa's just stoking it. Don't stay outdoors too long. Never know when there'll be another air raid.'

Fran blinked at the woman's astuteness and then again at her rapid switch in lucidity. Obviously the woman had fairly questionable mental faculties. 'A fire sounds…lovely,' Fran said carefully. 'How about you join me?'

'What?' The lady looked wildly at her. 'No, no, I can't. The children, I've lost the children. Little devils are always running off. I have to find them.'

Fran was saved further intervention by a young woman in a uniform who hurried up to them.

'Ethel, it's OK. The kids are still at school. It's not time for them to be home yet,' she said.

She was gentle and kind with Ethel and she winked at Fran.

'Oh? Really? Goodness me, I thought it was later than that. Better go get their tea ready, then.'

'That's the shot,' the woman said as she

escorted Ethel back inside and Fran followed. 'You are a full-time job,' she chided the old woman good-naturedly as they entered the imposing white building. 'You sure keep me on my toes.'

Ethel cackled and said, 'Gotta keep you young 'uns guessing.'

Fran was grateful to get inside. It was a typical sunny Queensland winter's day outside, but as Fran had no natural body insulation anymore, she always seemed to feel cold.

'Can I help you?'

Fran turned to see a glass window to her right that had a reception sign mounted on the counter. The woman who had spoken sat behind it and assessed Fran curiously. She was a short, thin, mousy woman with a pair of granny glasses perched on her nose and a drab cardigan. She reminded Fran of the stereotypical image of a librarian. Or a stern old-fashioned schoolmarm.

'Ah, yes,' Fran said, and gave the receptionist a small smile. 'I have an appointment to see Glenda Hopkins.'

'Sit over there.' She indicated the chairs against the opposite wall and picked up the phone.

Fran felt like she'd been caught smoking behind the bike sheds at school and was waiting to be called into the principal's office! But she sat because whoever the receptionist was, it didn't take Fran too long to figure out that she ruled the roost.

'Matron will see you now. Up the stairs, turn left, office at the end of the corridor.'

Matron? Fran got up as another wave of dizziness hit her. Matrons had gone out years ago. Was this the kind of place she would be working? Where a stern receptionist and a woman who insisted on using an ancient title ran the show? She felt her convictions wane. She didn't need the job that badly!

Fran's stomach growled again and she was almost sick with nerves as she knocked quietly on the door. Maybe this wasn't such a good idea after all. Fran heard a voice commanding entry and she took a deep steadying breath. She couldn't back out now.

The first thing Fran noticed was the absolutely gorgeous view from floor-to-ceiling windows. The office fronted the ocean and the one-eighty-degree views were to die for. The room was very spacious and Fran wondered if it had been one of the suites many years ago.

'Fabulous, isn't it?'

Fran dragged her eyes away from the view and took in Glenda Hopkins. She was nothing like the matron she had imagined. Sure, she was plump with a great big bosom but that's where the similarities ended. Her cheeks were rosy and her eyes twinkled and a huge smile was spread across her face, dimpling her chin.

She looked about fifty, not ninety-six as Fran had imagined, and…friendly. After worrying she was going to be one of those horrible cold crones from her student nurse days who had made their lives miserable, Fran wanted to go right over to Glenda and hug her.

Glenda burst out laughing at the surprised look on Fran's face. 'Not what you were expecting, huh?'

'Not exactly, no.'

Glenda waved her in and led her over to three wing chairs in an alcove near one of the windows. A small coffee-table sat in the middle laden with a tray carrying a tea pot, teacups and a plate of chocolate biscuits.

'Don't mind Catherine. She looks scary but she's a doll when you get to know her.'

A doll? Well, now, that would be an interesting metamorphosis to witness!

'She's just a little formal with outsiders and a bit set in her ways, but she runs this place very efficiently. I'd be lost without her, frankly.'

Fran nodded, wondering how long she had to work here before she wasn't considered an outsider. She was afraid to ask in case the answer was given in decades.

'I'm Glenda Hopkins, the director of nursing.'

Glenda stuck her hand out for Fran to shake and tried to hide her surprise now she had a close-up view of her prospective employee. Something bad had happened to Fran Holloway. She was the saddest-looking woman Glenda had ever met.

And that was enough for Glenda. She knew even before she'd seen any paperwork or spoken to Fran that she was going to hire her. 'Have a seat.'

As Glenda poured some tea and conducted the interview, her conviction became clearer. Fran Holloway needed them. It was as plain as the nose on her face, even if, in lots of ways, Fran was quite wrong for the job.

Oh, it was obvious that Fran was a competent nurse but she'd not worked in two years and didn't seem to have a glowing passion for geriatrics. It had been Glenda's unfortunate experience that city hospital nurses didn't tend to do well in a geriatric setting.

But it didn't take a genius to figure that something really awful had been responsible for her sabbatical and ultimately, to Glenda, it didn't matter anyway. What mattered most was that Fran needed these oldies much more than they needed her. She just didn't know it yet.

'So, what bought you to Ashworth Bay?' Glenda asked.

Fran looked over the rim of her teacup and gripped the handle tightly. 'I…needed a change and I've always wanted to live by the sea. When I saw the cottage on a website, I just…knew it was for me.'

Glenda digested Fran's evasive answer. There were worse reasons. 'So when can you start?'

Fran blinked. It couldn't be that easy surely—they'd only been talking for a few minutes. 'Ah… tomorrow?'

Glenda laughed, a big booming noise that curiously made Fran feel at home. 'Didn't you just say you'd only moved in today? I think we can give you a little more time.'

'Wednesday?' Fran asked.

Hmm. She was keen. Or desperate? 'Wednesday it is.'

They chatted for a while as they finished their tea. Glenda offered Fran a biscuit but she declined, too churned up to eat, and listened as her new boss ran over the general running of the place and the routine.

A knock at the door interrupted their conversation. It opened before Glenda invited whoever it was in.

'Gossiping about me, Glenda?' said a male voice with a gentle teasing tone.

Fran's back was to the door and she couldn't see their visitor but she did know the voice.

'Hah! You wish, David Ross. Come here and meet our newest recruit.' Glenda waved him over as she poured him a cuppa. 'Dr Ross is Ashworth Bay's only GP. He pops in every afternoon after his clinic is finished,' she explained to Fran.

David Ross? Her nextdoor neighbour, Miranda's father, was a doctor? Ashworth Bay's Nursing Home's doctor?

David drew closer until he stood beside Glenda's chair. 'Fran!'

Her sad eyes watched him warily and he bit back his effusive response. He took the chair beside her, deciding to approach her carefully, like one would a wounded animal.

'David,' she murmured. He was wearing dark grey trousers and a light blue shirt. The top two buttons had been undone like he'd just removed a tie. He looked nice and gave her a friendly smile.

'You two already know each other?' said Glenda, looking from one to the other.

'Fran just bought the Keegans' place,' he explained.

'Goodness, what a coincidence! You're neighbours.' Glenda beamed at them, shrewdly noting their lack of enthusiasm. Hmm…they were neighbours. Her mind raced with possibilities. Goodness knew, Miranda needed a woman in her life. And David—well, he definitely did!

David saw the speculative gleam in Glenda's eyes. She had been his practice nurse until two years ago when Matron James had retired. Glenda's parents' health had been declining and she'd needed a less demanding job. She had seen him at his best and most definitely at his absolute worst. He knew how she thought and he shot her a warning look. She beamed at him and winked.

'Small world,' said Fran, forcing a smile onto tight lips.

'Fran starts on Wednesday,' said Glenda, watching their interaction closely.

'Well, I'm sure you'll love it here,' he said kindly, helping himself to his third biscuit.

Fran nodded politely. 'Is there anything else you'd like to know, or are we finished?' Fran asked Glenda. 'It's just that I have such an awful lot to still do today….'

'Of course, my dear,' said Glenda, standing. David and Fran stood also. 'You go back to your boxes and I'll see you at eight on Wednesday morning.'

Fran felt the familiar dizzy sensation assail her as she shook Glenda's hand and forced herself to concentrate on not swaying.

'Are you OK?' Glenda asked as her newest staff member turned a shade paler, which Glenda wouldn't have thought possible until that moment.

'Of course,' said Fran dismissively, and turned to leave. As she took her first step the room began to shrink as an encroaching black cloud fogged her vision. Her legs buckled and she began to crumple to the ground.

David caught her just before she banged her head on the floor.

'Oh, David!' exclaimed Glenda, pressing a horrified hand to her mouth. 'What on earth is wrong with Fran?'

David swept a feather-light Fran into his arms and strode next door into his examination room. He laid Fran on the high narrow couch, a worried Glenda in tow. Fran murmured as her body came into contact with the cold, hard couch. Glenda hooked up an oxygen mask to the wall supply above the bed and put it on Fran's face.

'She just fainted,' David murmured as he watched Fran's light blue eyes flicker open and closed a few times. 'Let's get a blood sugar,' he said to Glenda.

'Ahead of you,' she said reprovingly, handing him the glucometer.

Fran felt the brief sting as the lancet pierced

her skin and the pressure of David squeezing her finger.

'Ow,' she murmured, opening her eyes momentarily, confused as to her whereabouts. 'What are you doing?' she said to David as a drop of her blood landed on the test strip. She sat up and pulled off her mask.

'You fainted,' he said. 'I'm taking your blood sugar.'

'I'm fine,' she said, swinging her legs over the edge and shutting her eyes as another wave of dizziness assaulted her. 'I'm often dizzy. It's just a bit of postural hypotension.'

The glucometer beeped. It read 1.2. He held it up so she could read it. 'When was the last time you had something to eat?'

Hell! One point two—no wonder she felt light-headed! Fran searched her memory. 'Um...last night?'

He heard Glenda's gasp as he pressed on. 'Are you a diabetic?'

'Of course not.'

'Glenda, get Earl to prepare something, will you?'

The director of nursing left, tutting. David smiled after her. Going a few hours without food was something he knew Glenda would never have contemplated. But, then, Glenda had led a blessed and happy life.

'Please, don't worry. I'm really not hungry,' said Fran.

David pointedly tapped the screen. 'Look, Fran,' he said gently as he took her finger and wrapped a sticking plaster around the puncture site. He sought out her sad, sad, eyes and continued softly, 'I know what it's like to feel so wretched that eating is a chore you'd rather not bother with. Really, I do know.'

Fran was caught and held by the note of sincerity in his voice and the compelling flicker of pain in his eyes. The same pain she saw when she looked in the mirror. She felt grateful for a moment to have found another human being who could at least begin to understand the depth of her despair. It was a blissful respite to not have to explain—not that she would have anyway.

'Look, I know my BSL is a little on the low side but, honestly…it's been a hectic day. I just didn't have time to eat. And, anyway, it was more likely to be my blood pressure. It's always a little on the low side.'

David nodded. He took the BP cuff down from the wall and quickly established her blood pressure was a little on the low side. But, of course, there was another possibility.

'Could you perhaps be pregnant?' It would certainly explain why a non-diabetic had such low blood sugar. And it could also explain her emotional state. Was she pregnant and all alone in the world? Had she been dumped? Or had she walked away from an untenable situation?

Fran felt a ridiculous urge to laugh hysterically. She could feel the bubble of inappropriate emotion rising in her chest and when the noise came it out it sounded more harsh than she'd expected. 'Hardly.'

'You sound pretty definite. Are you sure?'

'How about the last time I had sex was two years ago?'

David smiled and nodded. 'Yep. That's pretty sure.'

Fran laughed and David looked so startled that she laughed again.

'You should do that more often,' he said quietly when she'd stopped.

'Haven't had a whole lot to laugh about lately,' she said, her face sobering.

'Hmm. Yes, I figured. Time to start taking care of yourself, Fran.'

They looked at each other and at that moment Glenda pushed the door open.

'Earl's got some lovely pumpkin soup and crusty bread. He's even got some leftover steamed syrup pudding from lunch,' she said, sitting the laden tray on David's desk.

Fran felt her stomach revolt at the very thought of eating but David tapped the glucometer. 'OK,' she sighed grudgingly, 'I'll have something.'

David held out his hand and helped her down

from the high couch. 'You OK?' he asked as she leaned against him briefly.

No, she wasn't. Her daughter was dead. Her marriage was over. Her life had completely fallen apart and she was only thirty-seven. She definitely wasn't OK.

She nodded and let go of his supportive arm. She wasn't the only person in the world who had been dealt a bad hand. If she wasn't mistaken, David Ross definitely had history! But moping about it for the last two years hadn't got her anywhere—except for a blood sugar of 1.2 and a wardrobe full of clothes that didn't fit.

So maybe he was right. Maybe it was time to start taking care of herself. She couldn't heal her broken spirit if her body was broken, too.

Glenda left and Fran picked up her spoon, very aware of David's gaze. 'Are you going to watch me?' She felt like an anorexic teenager being watched like a hawk.

'Yep.'

David sat opposite her and drummed his

fingers on the desktop. She sighed and shook her head at the small smile playing on his lips, and when she grudgingly returned it, it became a face-splitting grin.

The food did smell delicious and tasted divine, but she couldn't do it justice. With her stomach unused to such large portions, she wasn't keen to test its limits. She pushed the half-finished soup aside and was just attempting dessert when he spoke.

'So, what's the Fran Holloway story?'

Fran paused in mid-mouthful and just looked at him. Telling him to mind his own business was on the tip of her tongue. Did he really think she would unburden her tale of woe on him? A complete stranger and her new neighbour? Even if his eyes told her he would understand, that he'd been through some pretty awful stuff, too? The urge to tell all gripped her unexpectedly and for a brief moment the thought of doing so appealed immensely.

'Come on, Fran,' he said gently. 'It's obvious to anyone with eyes that you've been through a rough time. Hell, even Mirry noticed. Maybe it would help to talk.'

'I don't know you,' she said quietly, trying to fathom why she was a nanosecond away from telling him everything. His gaze was gentle and compelling and she was, oh, so tempted.

'No, but I know you. Or your pain anyway. I can recognise an injured soul when I see one. Trust me, I know how easy it is to lock it away and bury it inside, but I also know how destructive that is.'

Fran just stared at him, letting his words wash over her. She felt tears prick her eyes and she looked down at her plate. It had been destructive for a long time but she was finally attempting damage control. Still, it was too early to talk about it, no matter how tempting he made it.

'It's OK, Fran,' he said, watching her downcast head and cursing himself for pushing. 'When you're ready, you know where I live.'

She looked up and he gave her a gentle smile. She nodded, too emotional suddenly to speak. It was a generous offer to extend to someone he barely knew and although she had no plans to take him up on it she was touched by his kindness.

'Eat up now,' he said, standing to go, 'or I'll send Earl in to spoon feed you.'

He grinned at her and it was exactly what she needed to balance the emotional see-saw that still swung crazily up and down inside her.

An open invitation to talk whenever she wanted. How different that was to claustrophobic but well-meaning family and friends back in Canberra who were constantly in her face, worrying abut her and checking on her. Nagging her that she wasn't eating and that she should be working and that she should go to counselling because it had been two years and she should be over it by now.

They'd meant well but Fran had been suffocating and at screaming point. David's no-pressure approach, his gentle understanding was exactly what she needed. Even if it wasn't any of his business!

CHAPTER THREE

A KNOCK on the door at seven-thirty on Wednesday morning startled Fran. She'd just stepped out of the shower and padded barefoot to the door, Fonzie at her heels.

'Who is it?' she asked as she approached, pulling the lapels of her towelling gown closer.

'It's David and Miranda.'

His rich tones seeped through the wood and Fran hesitated before opening the door. She wanted to flee back to the safety of the bathroom. Please, leave me alone, she wanted to say.

But she didn't. She opened the door instead. Miranda held a small basket with a checked cloth draped over the top. Fonzie barked excitedly at their visitor and leapt up, his paws on Miranda's thighs. She giggled.

'Ah, Miranda thought you might like some freshly cooked muffins for breakfast,' David said.

She dragged her eyes away from Miranda and Fonzie and noted David was dressed for work. He had on dark trousers and a crisp white shirt. Unlike Monday, he was wearing a tie. And what a tie! Hot pink, with yellow canaries decorating it. Fran blinked at the loudness of it and he shot her an embarrassed grin.

'Mirry is in charge of buying my ties,' he said, fingering it sheepishly.

'It's my special job,' Miranda confirmed, her attention finally drawn from the puppy. 'I even get to choose which one he wears each day.'

'Oh,' said Fran, a little lost for something to say because it really was a most awful tie but it somehow made him more…manly. Let's face it, she thought, you had to be a really confident male to wear such an awful tie.

She realised suddenly there was something about David she hadn't noticed before. He was attractive. Oh, it wasn't an attractiveness that slapped you in the face. It kind of crept up on you slowly. It was the sum of his whole rather than any one feature. His kindness, his confidence. His easy grin.

Fran blinked. She was standing in her gown on her doorstep, having improper thoughts in front of her new neighbours. She should have been embarrassed but she wasn't. It had been two years since she'd been aware of anyone other than herself and her own dark, dark world. It felt good to be dragged out of it, if only for a while.

'Anyway,' said David, as Fran continued to stare at them blankly, 'you're obviously in the middle of getting ready for work, so we won't disturb you any longer.'

Miranda handed the basket over and Fran took it, pulling back the cloth. Four big, fat, delicious-smelling muffins stared back at her.

'Goodness!' she exclaimed. 'All for me?'

'Daddy said you fainted on Monday 'cos you don't eat properly and I said that's 'cos you were sad and he said Earl's gonna feed you up and I said I'd help, too…. You will eat them, won't you?'

Fran glanced at David who had the grace to look embarrassed and shrugged a what-can-I-say shrug. She looked at Miranda who seemed very earnest. Like she'd been given the most important job in the world and it was vital she did it right. A little frown knitted her reddish eyebrows together and Fran wouldn't have denied this little girl anything.

'Of course,' said Fran, smiling at Miranda and feeling her heart squeeze at the gloriousness of the child's answering grin. 'It sure beats the toast I was going to have. I think I'll have one now and take one to work with me.'

'They're blueberry. I made them all by myself, didn't I, Daddy?'

'Yes, darling, you're the best chef in the whole world.'

'Except for Earl, Daddy.'

'Except for Earl,' he agreed.

Fran watched as David hugged the little girl to his waist. A fog of emotion encroached from the pit of her stomach and she knew it would only be seconds before it reached her face. Her arms ached watching their embrace and Fran swallowed a lump.

She cleared her throat. 'Thanks, Miranda, I'm sure they'll be delicious.'

David smiled at her and she saw the relief in his eyes. He was very protective of his daughter—that much was obvious. The fact that she hadn't shut the door and told them to go away had obviously pleased him. Had he expected her to do that?

Every grieving cell in her body had demanded it of her but Fran knew even now, after such short acquaintance, Miranda was going to be a hard child to ignore.

'Well, good luck for your first day,' David said as him and Miranda backed down the path.

Miranda waved at her as she shut the gate and Fran found herself waving back instead of closing the door. She stood and watched until the mop of red curls disappeared from view.

Fran's first day at Ashworth Bay Nursing Home was eventful, to say the least. Just getting back into the swing of things, learning a new routine, familiarising herself with residents and a marathon drug round would have been more than enough but, alas, there was so much more!

Catherine greeted her with a frosty 'Sister' and handed her a locker key. Fran followed her directions and found five navy dresses hanging there, as Catherine had advised. She stashed her bag and climbed into one. It was a size eight and she noted how much it hung on her! She'd never been this thin! She'd always been a generous size ten.

Glenda showed her around and introduced her to all the staff. She sat Fran down in a chair facing the view in her office and gave her all the residents' notes to read. It took a couple of hours to wade through the charts and decipher their histories from the different handwriting and degrees of legibility.

When Glenda rejoined her, Fran fired the myriad questions at her that had come up as she had familiarised herself with the residents. Glenda went on to explain the home's routines and strategic plan.

Fran was surprised to find out that it had been acquired thirty years previously by the foresight of the local council to address the needs of the ageing population of the area. It had only ever been slated as a low-care facility due to the expense and difficulties of converting the hotel.

That unfortunately meant that residents requiring a higher level of care had to be moved to other establishments and away from their beloved bay. The locals had fought for years to get the nursing home upgraded but there weren't the resources or people required to staff such a facility and not enough political clout to force the issue.

Earl came in and plonked a steaming mug of hot chocolate and a heavenly piece of cake in front of her.

'I insult easily,' he said, winking at her. 'Make sure it's all gone by the time I get back.'

Fran doubted, looking at big jolly Earl with his round belly and ruddy cheeks, that anything would insult him. It was hard to believe that he was married to Catherine, who would have to have been his complete opposite.

As she bit into the fluffy sponge she admitted it was nice to be taken care of for a change instead of trying to go it alone. She acknowledged as she ate his offering that a lot of her weight loss was due as much to apathy as grief. It was hard to be motivated to prepare something when there was just her. It had been a bit of a vicious circle really. Unable to stomach anything coupled with disinterest and lack of motivation. Combined, it had been a dangerous precedent for her health.

After lunch Glenda took her to meet the residents. They were an eclectic bunch. There was Mabel, the ninety-nine-year-old matriarch who was hanging out for her telegram from the Queen. Molly, Dolly and Polly, the eighty-two-year-old Ibsen triplets, who knew all the gossip, both past and present. Sid, who suffered from presumed peptic ulcers but was the bane of David's life because he refused treatment. And, of course, Ethel…to name but a few.

Fran's head spun with all their names and faces but Glenda assured her it'd take her no time at all to get to know them. 'A few pill rounds and you'll know them inside out and back to front.'

The first catastrophe occurred early that afternoon. Ethel went missing.

'What do you mean, she's missing?' asked Fran of Julie, the care assistant who'd rescued Ethel the day of her interview. 'Have you looked everywhere?'

'She's not in any of the usual places,' Julie assured her.

'Does this happen often?'

'She's never gone completely missing before.'

Great! She'd been here for half a shift and she'd already lost a resident! How was she going to explain that one to Glenda?

'Right, well, we'd better look for her. Have you searched the grounds?'

'Not all of them. Should we tell Glenda?'

'Lets do a thorough search first. Come with me.'

Bill, the gardener, helped them search every nook and cranny of the extensive grounds. Fran nearly had a heart attack as she followed the sturdy railing along the fenced cliff face, thinking about Ethel somehow managing to slip over the edge. Where was she?

'I'll go down the drive and check out the road,' said Fran to Bill, her heart thumping madly in her chest at the awful possibility that a senile escapee was wandering along the treacherous coast road. If she couldn't be found, Fran was going to have to get the authorities involved.

She reached the road at the end of the drive and looked both ways. Which way should she try first? Up or down? Fran felt sick, looking at the road. It reminded her of the roads you saw in European movies that hugged coastal cliffs with a sheer drop on one side. One wrong footfall on the shaly edge could be very perilous indeed.

A car beeped at her. David was in it. The window slid down. 'Walking out already?' He grinned.

His voice was light and teasing but Fran was too worried to notice. 'Ethel's gone missing. You haven't seen her on your travels, have you?'

David looked at the concern in her blue eyes and the way she chewed nervously at her bottom lip. 'Get in,' he said, reaching across and opening the door.

Fran sank into the leather seat of his Saab and buckled up, grateful that a set of wheels would hasten their search.

'She'll be fine,' David soothed, noting Fran's barely concealed worry making her even paler. 'Ethel grew up in these parts. She knows this road like the back of her hand. She's probably on her way to the school. We'll catch her up.'

Fran felt cheered by his words and smiled at him. 'Hurry, OK?'

They found Ethel a couple of kilometres away, sitting beside the road.

Fran leapt out even before the car had come to a stop.

'Ethel! Ethel, are you OK?' Her hands were covered in blood and Fran automatically thought the worst. 'You hurt yourself. What happened? Where are you hurt, Ethel?'

Ethel smiled at her blankly and looked at her bloody hands. 'Oh, dear, must be my sore knee. Silly me, I slipped,' she tutted, and smiled at Fran again.

David calmly got his bag out of the boot as he watched Fran frantically doing a head-to-toe check on a bemused Ethel. He crouched beside them. 'Ethel, my lovely, just where were you going on this fine day?' he asked and was rewarded with a flirtatious smile.

'Knock that off, young man,' she cackled. 'I'm married with kids. I was just picking them up from school.'

Fran felt her heart rate settle as the bump to Ethel's knee seemed to be the only damage she had sustained from her tumble. Her palms had a little gravel rash where she'd obviously put her hands out to break the fall. It was a wonder she hadn't broken anything, although the gash on her knee was still oozing blood.

'I think it'll need suturing,' Fran said to David.

She watched him as he calmly inspected the injury and chatted with Ethel. She delved in his bag for some gauze and saline so David could better assess the damage.

He looked at her and smiled. 'You're right. Let's get a bandage on it and get her in the car. I'll stitch it straight away.'

Ethel went quite happily, her hurry to pick up her kids forgotten already. They had her safely back at the nursing home a few minutes later, much to everyone's relief. Fran thought she even saw a flicker of emotion on Catherine's face as Ethel walked through the door.

'I'm sorry,' she said quietly to David as she helped him with the minor suturing procedure. 'I guess I panicked a bit.'

He smiled at her behind his mask as he pushed the curved needle through Ethel's anaesthetised skin, drawing the jagged edges of the long laceration together. 'No drama,' he said.

Despite his facial features being obscured by his surgical mask, she could see his smile reflected in his incredibly blue, incredibly expressive eyes. 'All I could think was how bad it would look, losing a patient on my first day, and that I needed this job and I didn't want to be sacked.' She snipped as he completed another suture.

David laughed and the richness of it caused Ethel to stop her humming and look at him. 'Is the job that important to you?'

Fran looked at David over the top of her mask and their gazes locked. Two pair of blue eyes, one light, like blue ice, the other deep, like sapphires, stared at each other.

Yes, it was. She may have only been there for a morning but getting back to work had been an essential part of her journey towards healing and she had enjoyed it. Well, until Ethel had decided to go walkabout anyway. She had felt useful and like her life had purpose again.

She had always loved being a nurse and had been really good at her job. And it had been great for a whole morning to be completely absorbed in something else other than herself.

'Yes,' she said quietly, holding his gaze, 'Yes, it is.'

They continued to stare at each other for a

moment more, and he nodded his head. 'Working helps,' he agreed. She nodded back and after another moment he got back to the job at hand.

He placed three more stitches and dared to push a little more. 'Glenda says you're from Canberra.'

Fran paused momentarily and then snipped again. Even mentioning the name of her home town conjured up painful memories. She flicked her eyes up but he had his head down, concentrating on the procedure. 'That's right,' she said.

'Long way from home,' he said quietly.

She shrugged. 'I've always wanted to live by the sea,' she answered noncommittally.

'Batemans Bay is closer, surely?'

She looked at him again and this time he looked back. His eyes were telling her it was OK to talk to him. 'Too close,' she murmured.

'Marriage break-up?' He'd already pegged her for that anyway. He could still see the faint ring mark on her unadorned ring finger.

She steeled herself for the usual storm of emotions. If it had only been that simple. 'Something like that,' she admitted evasively

'Messy, huh?'

'Awful.' She nodded and looked down quickly as she blinked away the tears she felt pricking at her eyes when she thought about all she'd been through in the last two years.

'I'm sorry,' he said gently, looking at her downcast head, having not missed the shimmer in her eyes.

David continued the job and let the matter drop and Fran was thankful to him. It was amazing how powerful a simple 'Sorry' could be, especially when it came from someone who had so obviously known his own share of grief.

'Come on Eth, your soap's on soon,' said Fran, helping her down from the procedure table a few minutes later. She took Ethel's soft wrinkled hand and led her to the communal television room. David followed.

The Ibsen triplets looked up from their card game and beamed at David as he walked through the door.

'Dr Ross, lovely to see you,' said Molly.

'Three times as lovely for me to see my favourite women,' said David, shooting them one of his easy smiles. They smiled back at him and Fran couldn't believe that three elderly spinsters could turn into blushing girls.

He chatted with the group of women that had gathered to get their daily dose of their favourite soap opera and requested they fill him in on the latest twists and turns. Fran sat for a while, her hand resting on Ethel's crinkled one and absently stroking it, relieved that she was safely back with them.

Ethel smiled blankly at her and nodded every now and then while her free hand polished her handbag with a piece of cloth. According to Glenda, Ethel went through three handbags a year by eroding them with her constant worried rubbing.

How awful, thought Fran, to be in a constant state of anxiety over a family of kids who were now grown and flown the nest. To be stuck in an unfamiliar home when every motherly instinct she possessed told her she should be elsewhere, looking after her little ones. Fran felt a strange kinship with the old woman, intimately acquainted with the totally bereft feeling of empty arms.

David made his excuses a few minutes later and Fran nodded and checked her watch. She should be getting onto the midafternoon medication round.

With David gone from the room and a commercial interrupting the show, Dolly turned to her sisters and said, 'That man can put his boots under my bed any day.'

Fran stared at the eighty-two-year-old and tried not to look shocked.

'Fight you for him,' said Polly, and all three cracked up.

'Ladies, ladies, you're shocking the new girl,' said Glenda, coming into the room and reading Fran's amazed expression.

Dolly turned to Fran. 'Ah, just because I'm in my eighties, Fran, it doesn't mean I can't appreciate a man who's easy on the eye. Wouldn't you say, Glenda?'

'Oh, very easy on the eye, Doll. But it's not blatant or showy, it's just there. Kind of subtle.'

'He's reminds me of that actor…you know the English one that plays that dreadful American doctor?' said Polly, tapping her forehead for inspiration. 'You know, it's on Monday nights.'

'Hugh Laurie—isn't that the chap's name? A thinking woman's sex symbol,' Polly said, nodding sagely, and all three of them sighed dramatically.

'Such a shame about his lovely wife,' said Molly.

Fran dragged herself back from her astonishment at the sex-symbol comment. Shame? Wife? Fran had guessed there was some heartache in David's past.

'He really needs to find himself a nice woman. It's been over eleven years,' added Molly.

'Fran has moved in next door to David,' said Glenda, and watched as the three octogenarians slowly took her meaning. They turned their eyes on Fran, and Glenda almost felt sorry for her.

Fran shrank back in her chair and eyed them suspiciously as they looked at her as if she were the first mango of the season. Oh, no! She'd come to Ashworth Bay to get her life together. Not for romance. Fran doubted whether that would ever be possible again.

'I'll just see to those pills,' she murmured, and fled the room.

Medication rounds were huge. Sixty residents with the mean age of eighty-one and their associated age-related illnesses made for a marathon trip. Fran pushed the heavy stainless-steel trolley out of the drug room and cursed its uncooperative wheels. Glenda had assured her she would get more efficient at it as she became familiar with the residents and the trolley, and that the first few rounds were always daunting.

And she was right. The round was bad enough without disaster number two landing in her lap.

One of her first stops was Mabel's room. The resident was lying on her back on the bed, her face turned away from the door.

'Mabel, I have your tablets.'

Mabel didn't stir from her sleep. Fran almost let it go, almost put the cup with the medication in it on her bedside table and left her undisturbed. Surely at a whisper away from one hundred, Mabel was entitled to have an afternoon nap? But something compelled her to persist.

'Mabel,' she said, louder this time. Still nothing. She entered the room and shook Mabel's shoulder gently. Fran was quite concerned now as the old woman still didn't move. She rounded the bed to a most disconcerting sight.

Mabel had her eyes shut. She'd vomited and Fran's nose caught the putrid smell of regurgitated partially digested food. Her breathing was gurgly and sounded obstructed, the left side of her face was droopy and drool trickled unimpeded from her mouth down her arm and onto the bedcovers.

Fran called her name and tried to rouse her, using a firm sternal rub. It was no use. Mabel was unconscious and, by the look of it, had had a stroke. Fran felt quickly for a carotid pulse and was relieved when the bounding vessel thudded against her fingers.

Fran rushed to the corridor and ran up it until she came across Catherine. 'Catherine, Mabel has had a stroke. Get Dr Ross. Tell him to bring the portable oxygen.'

She raced back to Mabel's room. OK, think, Fran. Think. She could hear Mabel's obstructed breathing from the doorway and knew that's where she had to start. She pulled the bed, which was on wheels, away from the wall and knelt behind it, enabling her to adjust the position of Mabel's neck back to the midline.

Fran placed her fingertips just underneath Mabel's jaw line in such a way that she was able to give jaw support to maximise Mabel's airway. There was an almost immediate cessation of the obstructed breathing and Fran let out a pent-up breath.

'Don't you dare die, Mabel. If you want that telegram from Her Majesty, you need to hang in there.' Fran's voice was quiet but she was sure the desperation was more than evident. Please, don't die, not on my watch. I've already lost one resident—how will it look to also have a death? The last thing she needed was Glenda questioning the wisdom of her decision to hire her.

'You're having an eventful day, Fran,' said David from the doorway, noting Fran's pallor and worry.

'Oh, thank God,' sighed Fran, never more pleased to see him than she was right now. 'The deficit appears to be left-sided so it's a right CVA. Did you bring the oxygen?'

David entered the room and sat on the bed beside Mabel. 'I'll examine her first,' he said.

Fran watched with growing impatience as he undertook a methodic neurological exam. What the hell was he doing? Didn't he know that the first minutes and hours post-stroke were crucial? Mabel needed to be in an emergency care facility. She needed a CAT scan and maybe some kind of angiography or at least drug therapy that could reduce the size of the clot in her brain and improve her chances for a meaningful, maybe complete recovery.

OK, he was the only GP in a small seaside town and she'd been out of the loop for a while, but this was hardly cutting-edge information. Even he should be up on these treatments.

'Shall I call an ambulance?'

David took the stethoscope out of his ears. 'Why?'

Fran stared at him, nonplussed. Was he mad? 'Because she's had a stroke. She needs to go to hospital. She needs to get treatment.'

He looked at Fran's earnest face and noted the wisps of blond hair that had escaped the plait. 'Help me get her comfortable,' he said to Glenda, who had entered the room at that point.

Fran stood aside as they inserted a guedels into Mabel's mouth to protect her airway, stripped back the coverlet that had been vomited on, got Mabel comfortable in the recovery position and covered her up with a blanket.

Fran couldn't believe what she was seeing. They were tucking her in? David brushed past her and motioned her outside.

'I'll ring her family,' said Glenda, and left to do so.

'What the hell is happening? She should be getting into an ambulance.'

'She's ninety-nine, Fran. She has a living will that states she wants no heroic efforts in the event of a heart attack or stroke.'

'So...we just leave her to die?'

David looked at the disbelief on her face. He had seen it many times with doctors and nurses who had come from the hospital system. They were used to treating. Everything that came through their doors they treated, admitted or patched up and sent it home again.

Aged care medicine was different. Nursing homes were places where old people came to live out their last years with respect and dignity and to die amongst friends and people they knew and loved.

'We let her declare herself, Fran. If she improves over the next few days, we'll transfer her to the nearest base hospital for rehab. But the chances are she won't. She's had a large stroke. She's unresponsive and barely breathing. We'll start her on an IV to keep her hydrated and some morphine for any discomfort, but I expect she'll just slip away some time in the next twenty-four to forty-eight hours.'

'She'd stand a better chance in hospital.'

'She's ninety-nine,' he repeated again, gently because he knew how fragile Fran was underneath her indignation. 'They won't treat her aggressively, Fran. Better she die here. Ashworth Bay is her home. She was born here, married here, raised her kids here, buried her husband here and wants to die here. Not in some faceless city hospital.'

Fran swallowed. She knew too well how awful that experience was. 'But...'

'We've all got to die of something eventually,' he said softly.

Fran felt a ball of emotion rise in her chest. She looked at Mabel and shook her head to dispel the moisture that had formed in her eyes. He was right. At least Mabel had had a good long full life. She herself was witnessing the natural life cycle drawing to a close and it was as it should be. Old women like Mabel died. Unfortunately young girls like Daisy sometimes did, too.

Fran nodded, refusing to look David in the eye. She couldn't bear the compassion she knew she would see there. The same wretchedness of heart she had seen flicker in his eyes once before. The empathy from someone who had been there and done that.

She excused herself and almost ran down the corridor in her haste to get away.

CHAPTER FOUR

FRAN pulled herself together and continued the medication round as Glenda organised for Mabel's family to come and formulated an acute-care plan with the care staff to keep Mabel comfortable in her last hours. The round was therapeutic because it gave Fran something else to think about instead of her rather notable first day!

It had certainly been interesting and one she wouldn't forget in a hurry. But she was on the home straight now. What else could possibly go wrong?

Cue disaster number three.

'Hi, Fran.'

Fran stopped in her tracks. That little voice sounded remarkably like Miranda's. She turned. 'Miranda? What are you doing here?'

'Oh, I come here every afternoon. The school bus drops me here and Daddy and I go home when he finishes with the oldies.'

No. Say it wasn't true! Not only did she live next door to this little girl that reminded her too, too much of everything she had lost but she was going to see her every day at work as well?

'Oh.' Damn it, why? Was this 'torture Fran' day? Surely an aged care home was hardly the most appropriate place for a twelve-year-old to be hanging out?

'I love it here and Daddy says as long as I do my homework first and don't get under anyone's feet and mind my own business and don't listen to Molly, Polly and Dolly when they start talking about sex then I can come here. Otherwise I have to go to after-school care and this place is so much more interesting. Don't you think?'

'Ah…ah…interesting, yes. That's a good word for it.'

'Where's Fonzie?'

'At home.'

'Oh, won't he be lonely?'

Fran looked at Miranda's little face, a frown between her brows. Yes, she suspected he would be very lonely indeed but she'd been trying not to think about it. 'I'm not gone that long. He'll get used to it.' She hoped.

'I know,' Miranda said, an excited little gleam creeping into her green eyes. 'You should bring him to work with you. We had a house cat but she died a few months ago. She used to belong to me but I couldn't keep her any longer so Glenda said she could be the home's mascot and that way I could still visit her a lot. Oh, Fran, it's perfect, don't you think?'

Fran opened her mouth to say she didn't think so when Miranda was off again.

'I'm going to talk to Glenda about it right now.'

And she was gone before Fran could call her back. Disaster number four. Fran stared after her for a moment and shook herself into action. She'd better go and put Glenda straight. First she'd lost Ethel, next Mabel had had a stroke, then she'd realised she would be seeing much more of Miranda than her heart could possibly bear and now it would look as if Fran was trying to bring her pet to work!

Glenda, David and Miranda were sitting at the table where Fran had been interviewed when she reached the office.

'Fran, come in. Mirry's just been telling us her idea,' said Glenda.

'Ah…yes, sorry about that. She ran off before I had the chance to stop her.'

'Stop her? What on earth for?' asked Glenda. 'I think it's a brilliant idea. The residents have had a long enough hiatus to get over Roger's death. Pet therapy cannot be underestimated. They doted on Roger. A puppy is just the right medicine, especially as Mabel's death will be felt so keenly.'

David looked at the bemused expression on Fran's face. It looked like she couldn't quite believe she was being railroaded by her boss and a twelve-year-old girl. Well, welcome to his life! Glenda had been bossing him around since he'd arrived in Ashworth Bay fifteen years ago and Mirry…well, she had him twisted firmly around her little finger.

'What do you say?' asked Glenda.

It would certainly solve her problems with worrying about Fonzie while she was at work. And he would be spoilt rotten—he'd love it. 'Yes…I guess. Yes.'

'Oh, Fran.' Miranda ran to her and wrapped her skinny arms around Fran's skinny waist and jumped up and down against her. 'That's so cool, Fran. Thank you, thank you.'

Fran felt her breath freeze in her chest as Miranda's arms circled her. She could feel the excited beating of Miranda's heart against her, and the feel of the little body against hers was so exquisitely right, so achingly familiar she wanted to sweep Miranda up and hold her there for ever.

Instead, she stood awkwardly, careful not to touch, her eyes shut, waiting for it to be over. Because if she gave in, just once, she was afraid she'd turn into an addict. An addiction far worse than that for any drug. The hit you craved when you'd lost a child and only their feel and their smell were ever going to ease the craving. Miranda wasn't Daisy but it had been a long time since she'd held a young girl in her arms and she ached for it so badly she could barely breathe.

Glenda and David looked at each other. She raised one eyebrow at him and he shrugged back. Fran was holding herself so erect and stiff it was almost comical. It was as if Fran was afraid Miranda had some awful contagious disease or something.

Was that the reason why her marriage had broken up? Because her husband had wanted kids and she hadn't? Or they hadn't been able to have them at all and even being near a child was a too painful reminder of what she couldn't have? So many marriages broke up over infertility.

'Come on, Mirry,' David interrupted, 'let Fran go. Have you done your homework yet?'

'Not yet,' she said, smiling up at Fran before letting her go. 'Mr Finch was just finishing his afternoon tea. He's going to help me with my long division.'

'Well, I'm sure he's done by now. I'll come and get you in half an hour.'

'OK, Daddy.' Miranda gave him a peck on the cheek and skipped out of the room.

'Sorry about that,' David apologized. 'She's a little too spontaneous for her own good.'

Fran shook her head dismissively and sent him a small smile. 'It's fine.'

'And we all do spoil and indulge her a little too much,' Glenda admitted. 'She's grown up among adults all her life. We tend to forget she's only twelve.'

The phone rang and Glenda answered it, chatting briefly before handing it to David.

'It's Penny,' Glenda said, filling Fran in. 'She's the RN whose job you now have. She's having some contractions and she's a bit worried.'

Fran and Glenda watched the brief conversation.

'Penny thinks she's gone into labour. She's having a bit of a panic. She won't calm down. I'm going to go and see her. Can you take Mirry home with you and I'll pick her up on my way past?' he asked Glenda.

'Oh, David, I can't today. I promised I'd go straight to the lawyer's in Nambour to sort out Mum and Dad's affairs.'

'No problem. I'll see if Catherine can do it for me.'

'She and Earl are going to the movies in Noosa straight after work,' said Glenda. 'Maybe Fran could do it?'

Fran looked up, startled. OK…it was the simplest solution. Her shift finished in half an hour and she was going straight home. David could take his time and Miranda would just be next door when he'd finished. But the ache in her soul rebelled at the idea. She was getting too involved with her neighbours and she didn't think she should set any dangerous precedents.

'Oh, no, I couldn't impose,' said David quickly. 'I'm sure the staff won't mind keeping an eye on her for me.'

Fran shut her eyes and sighed quietly. It seemed churlish not to offer. He had helped her find Ethel after all and been wonderfully kind and caring with her. 'I'll take her home with me.'

David looked at her. She looked like she'd rather saw off her arm. 'No, it's OK. She can stay here till I'm done,' he said.

'Nonsense.' Fran forced a smile on to her face. 'It makes perfect sense for me to take her home.'

David wasn't sure. Of course it made sense but he'd have to be deaf, dumb and blind to not pick up on her reluctance.

'She's right,' said Glenda. 'It does make sense.'

'Are you sure?' he asked hesitantly. He didn't want to push the friendship so early in the piece.

Fran nodded.

'OK…thanks, Fran, I really appreciate this,' he said, picking up his bag. 'I hope I'll only be an hour at the most. Penny is a bit of a panic merchant, though, so…'

'She'll be fine, David. Just go.'

He had no doubt she would be and Mirry would be in girl heaven, especially having Fonzie to play with. He just wished as he looked at her resigned expression that she seemed a little happier about it. He shot her a grateful smile and left.

Fran followed shortly after. She checked on Mabel. She seemed to be breathing much easier now and her daughter and son and some grandkids and great grandkids had arrived. There were tears but also a lot of laughter and reminiscing, and Fran thought what a nice sense of family and love was flowing around the room.

Glenda introduced her to the afternoon staff and she handed over to them and went in search of Mirry. She found her in the lounge, playing cards with the Ibsens. Fran stood in the doorway and watched them from a distance.

'So, Fran has moved in next door?' said Dolly to Miranda.

'Yes,' said Miranda, playing her card. 'It's very exciting. She has the cutest puppy and she's so-o-o-o beautiful, don't you think?'

Fran heard the wistful note in Miranda's voice. She sounded like the ugly duckling, wishing she could be the beautiful swan.

'What does your daddy think?' asked

Molly, shooting a sly glance at her sister and playing her card.

'He thinks she's very pretty. He said she looks regal or she would if she wasn't so skinny. And she looks sad but I told Daddy that I could make her happy again.'

Fran felt her heart bang painfully against her ribs. Oh, to be a child and have everything seem so simple. So logical! Happy? Fran didn't think she could be happy ever again. And she hadn't come here to be happy. To function as a human being again, yes. But happy was probably stretching it.

'Maybe your daddy could make her happy, too, my dear,' said Polly to Miranda.

Fran's eyes grew wider at the cheek of the three ladies who were old enough to know better, involving a child in their matchmaking schemes. Luckily it seemed to have gone over Miranda's head. She ignored her banging heart and entered the lounge.

'There you are, Miranda. Where's your bag, sweetie? It's time to go.'

Miranda smiled at Fran and surrendered her cards. 'It's in Mr Finch's room. I'll just go get it.' She skipped past Fran, smiling at her again.

'Such a cute kid, wouldn't you say, Fran?' said Molly innocently.

'Adorable,' Fran agreed politely, refusing to be drawn.

'Do you have any kids, dear?' asked Dolly.

And there it was. The question she dreaded more than any other. Every time it came her way she felt a jolt of electricity sweep through her, scorching her insides as she relived all the intensity and emotion of Daisy's short life. From her long painful entry into the world to her quick devastating exit.

How did she answer that question? She still didn't know. No, she didn't have kids? Because she didn't. But it felt disloyal and like Daisy was dying all over again to deny her existence. Or admit that she had had a child once and face questions she didn't want to face and try and find answers she wasn't sure existed?

'No,' Fran said quietly, and sucked in a deep

shaky breath as the pain of her denial felt like someone was gouging out chunks of her skin. No matter how much misery there had been, she would never not have had Daisy in her life.

'Shame. They're so precious,' said Molly, oblivious to Fran's pain. 'Particularly that little miss. Her father raised her from a baby after her mother died. And when she was so sick…that was such a horrid time,' said Polly.

Fran felt a prickle stroke down her spine and bring her out of her churning inner turmoil. She turned to the gossiping triplets despite knowing it was none of her business.

'Poor lamb still has to take all those tablets, too. Still, at least she's alive and if that's what it takes…' Dolly let her voice trail off.

Sick? Tablets? Miranda looked very well. What had happened?

'About time she had a female in her life. David's done a marvellous job but…sometimes a girl just needs a mother.' Molly put the screws on this time.

Fran's thoughts snapped back to the conversation when she realised where these meddling spinsters were heading. She'd already been a mother and it had been the most rewarding beautiful experience of her entire life.

It had also been the most excruciatingly painful, soul-destroying thing she'd ever done. And she had no wish to repeat it.

Miranda chatted away quite merrily in the car on the way home. Fran only half listened. Her mind and body were still reeling from the events of the day and the information she'd gained in the last half-hour. So, Miranda had some illness that required medication and David was a widower. It was too much information for Fran and she wished she hadn't been privy to it at all. She wasn't interested in the lives of her neighbours. The less she knew the better.

And she'd faced the dreaded question, the first time she'd been asked since arriving here, and was suffering the inevitable emotional fallout. She felt drained and just wanted to get home and crawl into bed. Not entertain a child.

'Oh, look, there's Fonzie,' said a very excited Miranda, and Fran realised they were home. She pulled the car up in the driveway and Miranda exited quickly as soon as Fran turned the ignition off. She smiled, despite the torrent inside her, at the child's zest.

Daisy had been like that. Always on the go. She would have loved a puppy, too, but Jeremy had never been a dog person and they'd always found some excuse not to. If she had only known then what she knew now, she would have got sweet, sweet Daisy her puppy and to hell with what her father had thought. But, then, hindsight was a wonderful thing.

It was five o'clock and already the last rays of daylight were fading from the sky. The air was crisp and Fran heard the waves as she alighted from the car. She inhaled a deep breath of salty air and felt the tension knotting every muscle of her body ease its grip slightly. Her face and jaw ached from so much talking and smiling and she realised how little she did these days that her muscles ached from such simple everyday activities.

Being social had not been her lot since Daisy had died. In fact, most people who knew the before and after Fran would say she'd become downright anti-social.

Fonzie leapt up onto her dress and Fran felt her tension ease further. His eager little face was so endearing and his unconditional love for her was soul-warming. She hadn't been an easy person to love over the last couple of years and she hadn't realised how much she'd missed it until a little black puppy had given it so willingly.

He didn't seem to know or care about her baggage, he just loved her because she was his mistress. Because she fed him and walked him and shared her bed with him.

'Come on, you two,' she said, and smiled at Miranda. 'It's freezing. Let's go inside.'

The warmth of the house enveloped them and Fran went straight to the fireplace, kneeling at the hearth and quickly getting a fire going.

'Oh, I just love fires. Aren't they marvellous, Fran?'

Fran squared her shoulders and steeled herself for the company of this girl for a little while longer. She could do this. She'd been a mother to her own little girl not that long ago after all. 'They're the best,' Fran agreed, and smiled at Miranda. 'Are you hungry?'

'Starving!'

Fran laughed despite the painful stirring of memories. It *was* kind of hard to fill little bellies up!

'I had this great kid make me some muffins this morning,' said Fran. 'There are two left. Fancy one?'

Miranda giggled. 'Blueberry! My favourite.'

Miranda put out her hand to help Fran up off the floor. Fran hesitated, afraid to touch Miranda in case she didn't want to stop. But she saw the confusion on Miranda's face when she didn't immediately take her up on her offer and gave in. The girl's hand felt warm but strong and Fran made sure she let go as soon as she was fully upright again.

Fran made a cup of tea while Miranda ate her muffin, accidentally, and a lot on purpose, spilling crumbs on the floor which Fonzie eagerly cleaned up. They chatted about school and the beach and the nursing home and, of course, her father. Fran found Miranda utterly charming, her red curls so cute, and she knew Miranda was already worming her way into her heart.

'Can I have the other muffin, Fran?'

'Will your father mind? I don't want to get into trouble for spoiling your tea.'

Miranda looked sheepish. 'You're right,' she sighed. 'Better not.'

Fonzie, who had given up on finding any more crumbs because he'd eaten them all, was lying in front of the fire when he cocked an ear and then barked. David's car was pulling up next door.

'Daddy!' said Miranda, running to the front door with Fonzie, opening it and dashing outside before Fran had even got off the chair.

She went to the door to check that Miranda had made it safely home.

'Fancy joining us?' David asked, holding a bulging plastic bag in the air. 'It's Chinese.'

Fran was about to decline. Spending time in Miranda's company had been bitter-sweet and she'd had more than she could bear today. But Miranda had other ideas.

'Oh, please, Fran. Please, say yes. I'd be so much fun! Fonzie can come, too, can't he, Daddy?' She turned to her father with begging eyes.

'Of course,' he said. 'Look, you did me a favour. I'd like to repay you. Besides, this way I can report to Earl that you're eating.'

David grinned at her and she felt the involuntary upward pull of her lips and surprised herself by nearly laughing. He'd taken his tie off and undone his top button and looked casual and nice.

'Please, Fran. Please?'

How could she resist such a gorgeous girl? 'OK,' she agreed. 'I'll just get changed. We'll be over in a minute.'

Fran could hear Miranda's excited chatter as she shut the door behind her. She changed quickly into some old faded denims that were threadbare at the knees and slung an old red scarf through the belt loops to help keep them anchored to her hips. She pulled on a navy chunky jumper which was warm and gave her some bulk.

Lastly she pulled her hair out of its plait and finger-combed the waves crinkling it. She had such fine hair it was easily arranged. She looked in the mirror and realised this was the second time in a day she had done so. She'd been so used to not bothering to look, not bothering to dress in a way that she needed to look, that the action surprised her.

Miranda greeted her at the door and she was ushered inside, Fonzie on her heels.

'Hi,' said David.

He, too, had changed, and looked more like the guy she had first met on the beach—jeans and a cream bulky jumper. His dark hair was tousled and she could just see the shadow of stubble on his jaw. Glenda had been right…he had an X-factor that didn't strike you immedi-ately. A thinking woman's sex symbol Dolly had said, and perhaps she'd been right, too.

'Hi.'

'Would you like some wine?'

He indicated the barstool on the other side of the kitchen bench and she sat down. 'Ah...' She hadn't indulged in alcohol in a long time. Drinking was such a social thing to do and it was just one of the many things that failed to hold her interest these days. 'Sure.' she smiled. 'Why not?'

Fran looked around her at the cosy cottage and felt the warmth and love that had gone into it and noted the little feminine touches. Pot-pourri in pretty bowls on the window-sills. A vase of bright yellow sunflowers. A sun-catcher crystal that hung from the window in front of the sink that no doubt spun rainbows of light around the room when the rays of the sun hit it in the morning.

Photos of David and a woman happy and laughing, and the two of them with a baby and older photos of Miranda and David littered every available flat surface. So, this was Miranda's mother. David's wife.

He passed her a glass of deep red wine and the bouquet caressed her senses as she brought it to her lips and sipped it.

'So, you like Chinese, I hope?'

Fran smiled. Before her life had gone to hell she could have lived on Chinese food most happily. 'It used to be my favourite.'

'Not any more?'

'Well,' said Fran, looking down at her body dispassionately, 'I don't much enjoy eating these days.'

David nodded slowly as he dished up the food onto plates. She looked beautiful tonight. Sure, she could definitely do with putting on a pound or two but she looked healthier in just a few days than when he had first seen her on the beach. Oh, the sadness that cloaked her every movement was still there, but she actually looked…more aware of her surroundings. Like she was starting to wake from a long sleep.

He felt the urge to kiss her rise and knew it wasn't the right time. Not that it was even a sexual urge. It had more to do with comfort. To let her know that she wasn't alone and it was OK to lean on someone. Everyone needed that and he didn't know why but he just felt he was that someone for her.

Of course, any kiss would rapidly become sexual. There was something about Fran that had nothing to do with his feelings of protection and solidarity. He'd first felt it on the beach. The way a man reacted to a woman he found attractive. Like he had when he'd first met Jenny. An awareness of her as a member of the opposite sex.

He passed Fran a plate laden with delicious take-away food and called Miranda. 'Wash your hands, sweetie,' he said.

Miranda did as she was told. 'Can I watch *Neighbours* while I eat, Daddy?' she asked, appearing from the lounge room.

'Ah…'

'Please, Daddy?' she begged.

'OK, OK,' he said, handing her a plate.

David sat down at the head of the dining table with Fran at his left. They ate in silence for a few minutes.

'How did you like your first day?'

'Well, it was eventful.' She gave a half-laugh and he joined her.

'Yes, nothing like an absconded resident and a stroke to start you off.'

'I have to wonder what tomorrow will throw at me,' she said and crunched into a spring roll. She realised that, despite her less than great start, she was looking forward to tomorrow and felt vindicated. She'd just needed to force herself to get going again!

'How was the pregnant woman...Penny? Was that her name?'

'Oh, fine.' He grinned. 'She's a bit of a worry wort. They were just Braxton-Hicks'. I stayed with her till they settled.'

'How pregnant is she?'

'Thirty weeks. I have a feeling we'll be hearing a lot more from our Pen over the next ten weeks,' he said, and laughed. 'You know what they say about nurses and doctors making the worst patients.'

Fran nodded and turned back to her meal, already feeling full. She pushed her food around the plate disinterestedly. A painting behind David's head caught her attention and she realised that the walls of the dining area were practically an art gallery. There were seascapes hung everywhere.

'Who's the artist? Are they local?'

He hesitated. Not because the words to his answer hurt any more but because he knew how other people reacted. 'My wife painted them,' he said.

Fran stopped chewing mid-mouthful. *I'm sorry* sprang to her lips but she knew how inadequate the words were so she just nodded.

'Jenny grew up in Ashworth Bay. In fact, she was one of *the* Ashworths. She loved this area and painting was her joy. Before Mirry anyway.' He grinned.

Fran felt jealous. Not of Jenny but how

easily David could talk about her. When would her hurt ever get to a point when she could smile and laugh and tell people without it feeling so crippling?

She cleared her throat of the sudden ball of emotion. 'Is that her?' she asked nodding her head towards one of the many photographs.

He turned and looked at the photo she indicated. Fran watched as he smiled gently at it, his mind obviously remembering the day it had been taken and how happy she'd been. 'Yes.'

'She was very beautiful.'

'Yes,' he said quietly, looking back at her. 'She was.'

Fran didn't know where the next question came from. It was none of her business and really she hadn't realised she wanted to know until she asked. 'What happened?'

He shut his eyes and sighed and Fran wished she hadn't asked. 'I'm sorry...I shouldn't have asked.'

He opened his eyes and smiled a sad smile at her. 'No, it's OK. It's just that even after all these years it can still get you, you know? When you least expect it.'

Fran didn't know. Oh, she knew his pain, but for her there had been no respite from it yet. She was still in the middle of the maelstrom. The thought that she might one day be where he was now was encouraging.

'Mirry was six months old. Jen was tired a lot. But, then, pregnant women, new mums, breast-feeding mums are usually tired and we put it down to that. Miranda wouldn't have won any awards for best sleeper. She was a real night owl. Jen didn't complain, she doted on Mirry and loved being a mother.' He paused and fiddled with his cutlery.

Fran listened without moving. She barely even breathed. He had a look of such sweet pleasure on his face as he remembered his wife and she didn't want to disturb him. Then a frown knitted his brows and his eyes were full of pain as he looked at her and continued.

'I got home one afternoon from work and all I could hear was Mirry, screaming her little lungs out. I knew something was wrong straight away. Jen would never have let Miranda cry like that. But I didn't really think it was anything too serious, you know? I went into the nursery and Mirry was all red in the face. She had these big fat tears running down her cheeks and she had a really foul nappy.

'I called out to Jen as I picked Miranda up and I realised she'd obviously been crying for a really long time because she was doing that hiccupy crying where their whole rib cage shudders, and even though she stopped crying almost instantly, little sobs were still being wrenched from her.

'I changed her nappy quickly because Jen still hadn't appeared and I was starting to get a really bad feeling. All I could think was that Jen must have gone out, but she wouldn't have left the baby. It didn't make any sense…but it was the only explanation so I went searching, thinking I would find a note or something.'

He stopped and Fran heard the emotion colouring his voice.

'But I found her instead on the bathroom floor. She was dead. The autopsy said she'd been dead for about six hours. The doctor in me knew she'd been dead too long to help but I had to try…you know?'

He looked at her with a plea in his eyes and she nodded because she would have done the same thing.

'I called the ambulance, started resus, and all the time Mirry was screaming…but it was no use. They got her to hospital but…if it had been anyone else they would have declared her dead here in the house…'

At that moment, as he relayed his story and his pain shone in his eyes, Fran felt more connected to him than she'd ever felt to anyone. She reached across and put her hand on top of his, stroking her thumb back and forth against his skin.

David felt the message communicated by her touch. *I'm sorry. It's awful. What hell you've been through. I understand.* He placed his other hand on top of hers and smiled at her, grateful for her quiet presence.

'The autopsy revealed she had HOCM. Hypertrophic—'

'Obstructive cardiomyopathy,' Fran finished for him. A condition that was quite often genetic. Miranda? Was that why she was taking medication?

'She'd been tired because her heart muscle was getting progressively worse until…she had a massive heart attack that day.'

Fran didn't have to pry to know that David blamed himself. And she knew how that ate away at you.

'And you blame yourself.'

He looked miserable and nodded his head, his eyes fixed on their joined hands. 'Of course. I was her husband. A doctor. I should have been more alert, had her lethargy investigated, but…'

Fran felt tears well in her eyes and she didn't bother to dash away the one that rolled down her cheek. 'You weren't to know.'

David looked up at the husky note in her voice and was touched by her display of emotion. He gently wiped the tear away and cupped her cheek for a brief moment. Fran probably didn't need to hear his depressing tale when she was obviously far from over hers.

Grief was a long slow road. It had taken him a long time to get to the stage where he could talk about Jenny and not break down. Miranda had wanted to know more and more about her mother and in recent years the deep ache inside had lessened and he'd been able to recall all kinds of memories with a fondness that warmed and gladdened his heart instead of wounding it.

Fran would get there, too…eventually. He knew how it felt to be in a tunnel so dark there was no light at the end. But one thing he knew for sure—if you walked the road long enough and kept putting one foot in front of the other, you eventually got to the light.

'I know, I know.' He smiled. 'Rationally I know that. But in those dark days following her death I blamed myself constantly. Thank God for Mirry. If I hadn't been forced to focus on someone else's needs, I don't know what would have become of me.'

Fran felt the lump rising in her chest again. He was spot on there. When Daisy had died it had been as if her whole reason for living had suddenly been stripped away. She'd had no one who'd depended on her any more. Yes, there'd been Jeremy but he'd been an adult and she had been too mired down in grief to think of his needs at all.

She had often wondered over the last couple of years how different things would have been had they had another child. Like David, she would have been forced to keep going, caring for the other child, keeping busy and active and out of the pit of despair.

'I'm sorry,' he said, gently pulling his hand out from under hers, looking at her stricken face. 'Forgive me, I shouldn't have gone on. It was a long time ago. Your loss is obviously much fresher.'

David was being so nice and for the first time she felt the urge to unburden herself a little.

'No. It's OK.' She drew in a deep ragged breath. 'My divorce became final last month…. My husband… It's been hard….'

She wasn't strong enough to tell him about Daisy. She felt like she'd break down completely if she even uttered her daughter's name aloud and she just couldn't go there yet. Talking about Jeremy was hard enough.

He placed his hand back on top of hers because he realised how hard it had been for her to tell him and she looked so wretched. 'It hurts, doesn't it?'

Fran looked at him and felt more tears running down her face. She nodded because the lump in her throat was so big she couldn't even speak. He didn't know the half of it.

He cupped her face again and it seemed the most natural thing in the world to rest her head against his shoulder. He stroked her hair and she fought a major battle to keep her emotions suppressed. She choked on a few sobs and it was so nice to lean on someone she nearly let herself go.

But she couldn't. If she did then she'd cry all night, and it wasn't the time or place. Miranda was in the other room and although David knew intimately the weight of her grief, she barely knew him at all.

'All I can say is that it does get better. I promise you, it will.'

She'd heard those words so many times before from well-meaning people that she tended to not even hear them any more. But David's quiet assurance was nearly her undoing. At least he could speak with some authority. This was a man who had found his wife dead and his baby screaming eleven years ago. His positivity gave her something to cling to even though she knew her grief was twice as deep, twice as wide, twice as dark as his. She'd lost her husband *and* her child.

She pulled away to tell him so. He looked at her earnestly and she didn't think he'd buy the yes-but-my-grief-is-worse-than-yours argument. Death was death and grief was grief and no one person's was any worse than anyone else's. It all hurt and it all sucked and it was all so unfair. She wasn't going to diminish his by saying at least he still had Miranda.

David waited for her to say what she wanted to say. She looked about to say something important but he watched as she changed her mind and smiled and thanked him instead.

'You know you can talk to me. Any time. Day or night.'

'I can't,' she said. 'It hurts too much.'

He nodded because he knew the truth of her words. 'It won't always.'

'Promise?' she whispered. Fran just couldn't see that this pain was ever going to pass.

He smiled and put his bent elbow on the table, waggling his little finger at her. 'Pinkie promise.'

Fran stared at him for a few moments, the action stirring memories.

'Mirry swears by them,' he said, and waggled it, along with his eyebrows, again.

So had Daisy. It had been their little ritual when Daisy had sought any kind of reassurance. A pinkie promise in the eyes of a ten-year-old girl had been equal to, if not greater than, a vow written in blood.

He waggled it again and she gave him a grudging smile and linked her pinkie with his. 'Pinkie promise,' she murmured back.

They let their fingers linger for a few moments longer than they should have and Fran felt warm all over. She'd been so used to feeling cold all the time it was bliss to feel a momentary heat.

David felt the urge to kiss her return. They were quite close and she was looking at him with big sad eyes. He pulled gently on their joined fingers and dropped a light kiss against her mouth. A fleeting touch of his lips.

He pulled back to gauge her reaction. She blinked at him and he could see her grappling with what had just happened. He could see confusion in her eyes as she blinked at him again.

Fran dropped her finger and thought, get the hell out of here now. He'd kissed her and something inside her was stirring that shouldn't be. She was grieving, in mourning. Jeremy was gone. Her daughter was dead. It wasn't right to be having these feelings. He shouldn't have kissed her.

'I'm sorry,' he apologised quietly, watching her closely as she continued to stare at him.

'I'd better go,' she said, standing and scraping her chair back abruptly.

He stood too. 'Forgive me, I don't know what came over me. You looked so sad and—'

'I'm not ready for anything like this, David,' she interrupted. She shot him a firm look to make it clear. 'I don't know if I'll ever be ready.'

'Fair enough.' He held up his hands. 'It won't happen again.'

Fran regarded him seriously for a few moments and then nodded. 'I'd better go.'

David didn't protest. He didn't want her to go but he'd obviously rushed her and she was more skittish than ever. And if she'd felt what he had when they'd linked fingers and then kissed and, from her confusion, he was fairly certain she had, she was no doubt running a little scared, trying to work out her jumbled emotions.

As he watched Fran walk down the path he felt like he had made some real progress with her tonight, before he'd ruined it anyway. She'd obviously needed someone to lean on and he hoped she might just allow it to be him, eventually.

Sure, divorce was a complicated situation. It wasn't like a death where there was no choice. Divorce usually signalled several years of heartache. And grieving the death of a relationship was just as real and difficult as an actual death, especially if it was compounded by large amounts of guilt.

But he was coming from an area of strength. He understood probably even better than she did about grief and its implications because he'd come out the other side. Fran had so much going on in her head. Would she let him in, especially after tonight? One touch of her pinkie and her soft lips and he'd realised he wanted to be let in—very badly.

CHAPTER FIVE

MABEL DIED ON FRIDAY morning with her family at her side. Fran had heard them all singing 'Amazing Grace' as she had passed by, doing the medication round, and the hauntingly mournful notes had resonated into the hallway, raising the hairs on the back of her neck.

Tahni, one of her daughter's friends, with a voice like an angel, had sung the same hymn at Daisy's funeral. It had been like Tahni was floating Daisy up to the angels on the wings of her melody and there hadn't been a dry eye in the house.

Thankfully the next couple of weeks passed uneventfully at work. No one absconded. No one died. No one even got sick. Fonzie was revelling in his daytime role as house pet and it was a good, consolidating time for Fran. She got to know the residents and their families and her role. She was beginning to feel comfortable with what was expected of her and to make decisions herself, instead of asking for advice or following Glenda's lead. She felt her old confidence coming back and it helped to ease her transition back into a functioning life.

In fact, her work kept her so occupied during the day and so tired at night that Fran was surprised at how quickly time passed. The last two years had crawled by, each day longer than the last, wandering aimlessly around the house waiting for the night so she could go to sleep and forget for a while.

She didn't notice the weather warming up or her appetite improving or her clothes fitting better. She went to work, Earl fed her continuously, Miranda cooked her all sorts of treats and usually joined her in eating them. David, who took great pains to keep their relationship platonic, persuaded her to eat with them a few nights a week, too. He was an excellent cook and food actually started to taste better.

They fell into a routine that just kind of happened. Fran would bring Miranda home when David was called away or going to be late because it made sense and Miranda was hard to dissuade! Those were the nights Fran would go and eat with them. They were careful to not repeat their conversation of the first time they had talked. David figured when she was ready and it felt right, she'd talk.

Even having Mirry hanging around had lost its painful intensity. There were still the odd times, as David had described, when she did something, like twirl her hair around her finger, or said something Daisy-like, when a jolt of pain would unexpectedly stab her in the heart. But Mirry's fairly regular presence had taken the edge off Fran's extreme emotional reactions.

By the time her two months' employment anniversary had arrived, Fran was beginning to feel like a local. As she walked into the nursing home one morning, everyone greeted her warmly…well, except for Catherine, who still called her Sister and nodded formally, but Fran thought she detected a faint smile from time to time.

Fran smiled at Ethel, who gave her a vague grimace back. She had taken a real shine to the dementia patient. Fran knew it wasn't done to have favourites but there was something about the constantly worried old woman that spoke to her. Maybe as a mother who had lost a child she could better understand Ethel's panic when she realised her babies were gone.

How many times had she woken in a cold sweat with a bounding heart in a blind panic about Daisy's absence, only to realise the awful truth?

Fran fell into a routine of walking around the grounds with Ethel every morning, following the drug round. It was usually about this time of day that Ethel started to become agitated, worrying about her kids, and was most likely to wander. Fran found she could distract her quite easily as Ethel was an expert gardener.

Today wasn't any different. 'Come on, Eth,'

she said, guiding the worried old lady out the door with her, 'let's go for a walk. I need you to tell me about perennials.'

They wandered around the grounds for half an hour, Fonzie following them and chasing the occasional bird. Ethel stopped to give advice to Bill about his planting technique and pointed out areas where he had been remiss. He took it good-naturedly as always, and promised he'd get right onto it.

Ethel was telling her all about bulbs when she suddenly stopped and looked around. 'Do you know where my kids are?' she asked, looking Fran straight in the eye. 'They were here only a moment ago…probably playing hide and seek behind those great Moreton Bay figs. Little devils.' She chuckled and shook her head. 'You got kids?' Another piercing look.

Fran was so used to the question by now that it had lost its wounding impact. She'd been asked that question here at least twice a day. It was hard not to be asked in a home full of old people whose main focus was their grandchildren.

She'd found herself a standard reply that deflected curiosity and usually put it straight back on them by asking them about their grandkids.

Today, looking into Ethel's eyes that, for once, looked completely rational, she felt comfortable enough to tell her the truth.

'I did. A little girl. Daisy.' Her heart hammered like a train and she let out a strangled, pent-up breath. It actually felt good to acknowledge her daughter for a change.

'What happened?' asked Ethel, still lucid.

'She died two years ago.'

'Oh, dear, how awful for you,' she said. She picked up Fran's hand, brought it to her chest, held it close and patted it.

Fran's eyes welled with tears. 'Yes,' she said.

They stood in silence for a moment then Ethel smiled at her blankly, looking down at their joined hands. She gave Fran a confused, why-am-I-holding-your-hand look and let go.

'Come on, Eth, I bet Earl has some delicious biscuits just out of the oven.'

'Ooh. Biscuits…my favourite.'

Fran's step was lighter that day, bouncier than it had been for a long time. She'd confessed something she'd been holding close to her chest since she'd arrived in Ashworth Bay. And, surprisingly, she hadn't shrivelled up and died.

In Canberra everyone who knew her knew the tragedy that had befallen her, and it had felt claustrophobic.

People had either wanted to talk about it or hadn't, and she'd been unable to bear either. The talkers constantly opened the wound, tearing the sutures out with their bare hands. And the avoiders just made her angry.

Oh, she was grateful to them on many levels but, perversely, she had just wanted to yell, *Say her name, damn it. Daisy. Her name was Daisy!*

She'd escaped to Ashworth Bay to start a new life but also to get away from well-meaning family and friends. It was a triumph to be able to talk about her daughter. To speak her name without everyone holding their breath and waiting for her to fall apart. And she hadn't fallen apart. But she had needed to get there at her own pace.

Not that she was ready to start talking about Daisy to all and sundry. If it had been anyone else but Ethel she wouldn't have mentioned her at all. There was a safeness in confiding in someone with dementia. Ethel had forgotten her secret in less than a minute so there was no risk that she would gossip about it. The fact she was a divorcee had caused enough of a sensation and that was all she was prepared to share at the moment.

When David found her that afternoon she was sitting with the women who were watching their favourite soap opera. Ethel was in the recliner beside Fran, rubbing her handbag with her ever-present cloth, the Ibsen triplets were there and Miranda was in the thick of it.

Even Sid had been drawn into the lounge room at the gales of female laughter. He had sat silently rubbing his chest, a frown firmly in place. Fran had offered him some medication to ease the burning sensation but he had refused miserably.

'Good news, everyone,' David said as he entered the room. 'I've just heard from Penny. She had a baby boy last night. Seven pounds, three ounces.'

There was general excitement from everyone and the Ibsens started organising what to knit now they knew the sex of the baby. David winked at Fran, who was grinning at him. They'd not heard any more from Penny since that time a couple of months ago and he was relieved that she had seen fit to go straight to the hospital yesterday rather than call on him.

'Betty is first up for you today,' said Fran as she watched Mirry hug her father and climb onto his lap as David sat in his daughter's chair. She felt a little pang in her chest at their closeness and remembered how close Daisy had been to Jeremy.

'OK,' he said. 'I'll just watch to the ad break.'

Mirry snaked a finger into her curls and twisted one absently around and around as she watched the television. The gesture had far less impact on Fran now than it had early in their acquaintance. It was kind of nice to see it now and reminded Fran of happier days.

'I'll go get her,' Fran said, because suddenly she was feeling a little fragile emotionally.

David looked so comfortable with his life. He was wearing another awful Mirry tie—mission brown with cane toads all over it—but it didn't detract from his attractiveness. He looked nice and safe and warm and she suddenly envied Mirry. Being curled up on his lap looked like the best place in the world to be at the moment.

David gave Mirry one last squeeze before getting up. It was easy to forget with the elapsing of time how sick his little girl had been. He never wanted to take her for granted. 'Grandma should be here to pick you up for your sleepover soon. OK?'

'Sure, Daddy.'

She smiled her big, big smile at him and he got a chill up his spine, remembering how he'd so nearly lost her, too. 'You be good. Don't forget—'

'My tablets,' Mirry finished for him. 'Relax,

Daddy, I'll remember. And, anyway, Grandma won't let me forget either.'

David laughed. That was true. Jen's mother was fanatical about them. Marlene Ashworth had no intention of losing another member of her family and certainly not her only genetic link to her darling daughter.

He sat down next to Ethel to have a quick chat. Fonzie was lying in his usual spot at her feet. It wasn't just Fran who had developed an attachment to Ethel. Maybe the puppy instinctively knew that Ethel was a wanderer and needed to stick close? Or maybe he was just following his mistress's lead?

'How was your walk, Eth?'

'Hmm, dear?' she said, her blank eyes looking at David vaguely as her hand continued to rub at her bag.

'Your walk. With Fran?'

'Poor Fran,' she tutted. 'Losing her dear daughter like that.'

David's smile slackened for a second. Daughter? He shook his head. Ethel had dementia, she'd no doubt got her information all muddled. He smiled at her and patted her hand.

'Have you seen my kids?' she asked him.

Poor Ethel. 'They're still in school,' he said, and when she gave him a smile of relief he knew he couldn't feel guilty for his little white lie.

Fran called at Betty and Ted's room to fetch Betty. She'd been surprised when she'd first met Betty. She and Ted could often be heard bickering and Fran had expected a bit of a fishwife but she was the exact opposite—small and petite with elegant hair and beautiful nails.

'You ready for the doc, Betty?' asked Fran, sticking her head around their door. Betty and Ted were one of the few married couples at the home. The married accommodation was self-contained and almost double the size of the single rooms.

'She doesn't need the doctor,' Ted griped.

Fran watched as Betty shot him a look that would have done a Shakespearean shrew justice. 'Be quiet, Ted, you grumpy old man. I'm going and you're going to thank me for it.'

Fran raised her eyebrows at their ex-change—this sounded interesting indeed. She accompanied Betty part of the way and started to peel off as they passed the medication room.

Betty stopped her. 'Actually, Sister.' Betty was the only person other than Catherine who insisted on calling her Sister. 'Would you mind coming in with me to see the doctor? It's rather…personal and I'd feel better if I had another woman with me for moral support.'

'Of course, Betty,' said Fran, smiling reassuringly, 'Everything OK, I hope?'

'Yes, dear.' She smiled. 'Or it soon will be with any luck.'

Fran's mind boggled. Was it a female problem? Or something else?

It didn't take long to find out. Betty got straight to the point. 'I'd like some Viagra for Ted, please, Dr Ross.'

Fran swallowed her gasp of astonishment too late. Betty pierced her with one of her quelling looks. 'Just because we're in our eighties, Sister, that doesn't mean we still don't like to have some loving every now and then.'

'Of course not,' said Fran, suitably chastened, not even game to look at David.

'I mean, for goodness' sake, he couldn't keep the damn thing down when we were younger, but these days…well, let's just say the mind's willing but the body's not able.'

'Right,' said David, keeping a straight face lest Betty decide to become shrewish at him. 'Can I ask why Ted isn't here?'

'Oh, why do you think, Dr Ross? He's a man of a certain generation and you just don't discuss those kinds of things. Bloody stupid, I told him. Move with the times, I said.'

'Quite right,' said David, risking a look at Fran who was finding the ceiling exceedingly compelling.

'Would you like me to have a word with him?'

'That would be most satisfactory,' the old lady said. 'He will be a suitable candidate, won't he? We did an internet search on it and he doesn't have any blood-pressure problems.'

Fran raised her eyebrows at Betty. She knew they had a computer in their room but she'd just assumed it was there for the grandkids to play with when they visited. She winked at David.

'It could just be his diabetes, Betty. Let me talk with him. I'm sure we'll have you both back up to speed in no time.'

'Oh, thank you, Dr Ross,' said Betty, standing. 'I know it may seem silly and trivial and I don't expect the world, but every now and then…if the mood is good then it's rather a pleasant sleeping pill, wouldn't you say?'

'The best,' David agreed, and walked Betty to the door.

'Well, that's something you don't see every day,' he said as he shut the door.

'No,' said Fran, standing to leave, a grin playing at her lips. 'It's a first for me.'

They smiled at each other and Fran joined him by the door. They reached for the knob simultaneously. Fran felt his warm hand on top of hers and they both apologised together, but he didn't loosen his contact.

David cleared his throat as he looked down into her pale blue eyes. They looked so much more expressive than on the day he had first met her. 'I've been meaning to say how great you're looking these days, Fran.'

She nodded slowly and smiled a small smile. 'I'm feeling better. A bit more like a member of the human race instead of a…zombie.'

Zombie was a very apt description, David thought as a wispy piece of her hair fell loose from her braid across her face. He hesitated slightly before gently lifting it away with his index finger and tucking it behind her ear. He contemplated kissing her again but he'd lost so much ground last time he didn't want to risk it again.

Fran felt her breath catch in her throat. The small touch was gentle yet caused a squall of sensations inside her. Standing looking down at her was a man who had helped her more in two months than anyone had in the last two years. He was a kindred spirit and even though she knew it was wrong to have feelings for another man in the midst of her grief, she was attracted to him.

She licked her lips nervously and noticed how his eyes widened at her unintentional signal.

Oh, to hell with it! 'Fran,' he whispered as he lowered his head towards her.

His lips touched hers and they were so gentle, so compassionate she shut her eyes, afraid she might cry at the sheer beauty of its simplicity. But then they were moving away and Fran wondered for a brief moment if she'd imagined it. She opened her eyes to see him smiling down at her.

'Fran—'

They were interrupted by the door being opened in their faces, forcing them to step away quickly from each other to avoid injury. Glenda did a double-take and then eyed them suspiciously. 'I'm sorry, I didn't realise you guys were in here.'

'No problem,' said David, moving back behind his desk. 'Is there anything in particular you wanted?'

'I just wanted to grab a textbook,' she said, assessing Fran's pink cheeks. Fran hadn't had pink cheeks the entire time she had known her.

Sure, she wasn't so pale these days but…something had been going on!

'I'll leave you to it,' said Fran, and beat a hasty retreat. Now the kiss was over her heart was hammering a frantic tattoo. Oh, dear, what was happening? This wasn't good. It wasn't good. The first time he had kissed her even though she'd been confused she'd known she hadn't been ready, but now? Months later? It didn't seem so preposterous.

She was distracted from her careening thoughts by Fonzie, who barked at her. That was odd, Fonzie never barked inside. 'Shh, boy,' she chided gently, getting down on her haunches and giving him a pat. He didn't drop to the floor and roll on his back like he usually did and she wondered what was wrong. He barked at her again and trotted away.

She followed him because her gut said something was wrong. He picked up the pace periodically looking back at her to check if she was still coming. He disappeared into the lounge and Fran walked in after him.

When she arrived a few seconds later he was sitting at Ethel's feet, wagging his tail and barking noisily. Luckily everyone else had vacated the room now the soap had finished.

'What's up, boy?' she asked, and knelt in front of Ethel, displacing him slightly. 'Shh,' she said, looking down at him. 'You'll wake her up.'

Fran looked at Ethel, wondering how on earth she could sleep through the racket. OK, he was a puppy and he had puppy barks, but still...

Then she didn't have to wonder any more. Ethel wasn't rubbing worriedly at her handbag, she was still, her eyes closed. She looked asleep, her worried, lined face relaxed and peaceful. Fran felt a block of emotion well in her chest as she grabbed Ethel's wrinkled old hand and felt for a pulse. The skin was crinkled at the knuckles and was soft but it felt cold and Fran couldn't feel a pulse. She checked the carotid artery as tears welled in her eyes.

'Oh, Ethel, no,' she whispered, and looked down at Fonzie as tears spilled down her face and he whined at her. She scratched behind his ears and he looked at her with a kind of perplexed look on his face. 'I know, boy, she's gone. Ethel doesn't have to worry about her kids any more.'

Fran left Fonzie sitting at Ethel's feet and shut the door to the lounge. She took deep cleansing breaths as she made her way to David's office, afraid that the crush of emotion in her chest would bubble out uncontrollably and she'd falter and crumble before she reached her destination.

Glenda and David were still deep in conversation when Fran knocked and David's voice bade her enter. His quick easy smile died at her distressed look.

'Fran, what's happened?' He stood because he hadn't seen her look this wretched since she'd first arrived in Ashworth Bay.

Glenda pulled out a chair and Fran sank gratefully into it. 'Ethel's dead,' she said quietly, and battled the urge to let her face crumple and allow the threatening sobs a blessed release. She worked in a nursing home. People died. Even favourites.

Glenda looked at David. Neither of them were surprised but it was still sad when a resident died. 'You go and see her,' said Glenda above Fran's head as she wrapped her arms around Fran's shoulders and hugged her tight. 'I'll stay here.'

No, he wanted to say. You go. I'll comfort her. He wanted to be the one to hold her, to comfort her. Damn it! Fran needed this now like a hole in the head. She seemed to be finally starting the long journey back to living. Having to face another loss of someone she'd grown close to just wasn't fair.

But Glenda was right. He had official things to do. Declarations, phone calls and certificates. 'Is she still in the lounge?' he asked quietly.

Fran nodded and he came round the desk, knelt beside her and squeezed her hand. He noticed how cold it was before she quickly withdrew it, her face taut with unshed tears. He glanced at Glenda and she nodded at him to go.

He came back a few minutes later with a forlorn-looking Fonzie. Glenda moved and he plonked the black puppy in Fran's lap. She automatically stroked his thick coat, hugging him to her, and Fonzie licked her face.

'Why don't you go home, Fran?' suggested Glenda. 'There's only another half hour anyway.' Glenda looked at David for approval of his suggestion and he nodded at her.

'Good idea, Fran. Take Fonzie home. I'll call in on you later.'

She didn't argue with him. It was taking all her willpower to keep herself together. She drove straight home. The waves were calling her as she alighted from the car and she and Fonzie went directly to the beach. It was overcast, big dark clouds rolled in from the ocean, and Fran wondered if they were going to get some rain. The wind was quite cool and the brooding conditions shortened the time of available daylight.

Either Fonzie sensed something was up or was sad about Ethel, too, because for the first time he stuck close, rather than dashing about like a mad thing. He flopped on his stomach beside her, his arms and legs outstretched, his head between his front paws resting on the sand. They watched the flow and ebb of the waves that crashed in big rolling dumps against the beach. The sea was unsettled, white foam capping the choppy peaks, reflecting Fran's mood perfectly.

The wind picked up a notch as visibility worsened and the first sprinkle of rain chilled Fran's skin further. The sand beneath her felt cold and damp. Still she sat in the drizzle listening to the pounding rhythm of the sea, fighting back the emotion that roared like the waves inside her.

David found them there in the last dying light of the day, wet and shivering.

'Fran,' he whispered, crouching beside her.

She heard him but his voice sounded far away and she daren't stop concentrating on the rhythm of the waves because it was the only thing keeping her together.

David felt how cold she was and Fonzie whimpered at him, obviously concerned about his mistress. 'Fran,' he said firmly, and shook her shoulder. 'Come on, we're going back to the house.'

Fran turned to him then, his voice breaking into the almost hypnotic state she'd been in. 'I'm cold,' she said, her teeth chattering.

He picked her up in his arms and she huddled in the shelter of his warm body, absorbing his body heat gratefully. Fonzie followed them up the beach and straight into David's house. He wrapped a rug around her shoulders and sat her on a big old comfortable leather chair in front of the fireplace. He got a fire going until it roared around the room almost as loudly as the waves on the beach. Fonzie plonked himself near the hearth and promptly went to sleep.

David made her a cup of sweet milky tea and held it out for her to take. She was staring at the fire and he knew she was like a dam wall ready to burst. Her fingers accepted the hot drink and he watched her wrap her chilled hands around the mug and draw it close to her chest.

She shivered and David saw her pain and

grief in the slump of her shoulders and the shine of unshed tears in her blue eyes. Her hair was damp, hanging scraggily in dark, limp strips around her face.

They sat in silence for a while and drank their tea. David sat on the Persian rug on the floor beside her chair and when he'd finished his drink he put his cup on the coffee-table beside the chair.

He turned to her, sitting on his haunches in front of her. He noticed she'd barely touched her drink. 'You know you can let it out, Fran. It's just me.'

She shook her head from side to side, continuing her hypnotic gaze at the fire. 'I can't' she whispered.

'Yes, you can,' he said gently. 'I don't mind.'

Fran switched her gaze from the fire to his earnest face. 'I'm afraid I won't be able to stop.'

Her big blue eyes were large with fear. He prised the mug away from her stiff fingers and took both of her hands in his, rubbing them gently. 'Would that be such a bad thing?'

'I don't want to feel this way again.'

He nodded and brought her hands to his mouth and kissed each one gently. She was reminded of the fleeting kiss he had given her earlier that day.

'I know,' he said. 'I know.'

And Fran realised that he did know. He knew the gut-wrenching depths of grief and the first flutterings of hope as you began to see your way out of it. He knew how stepping back into the dark was too frightening for words.

She started to become aware of David's thumbs rubbing rhythmically against the skin of her hands. Her nipples hardened and her skin broke out in goose-bumps even though she was now actually quite warm. She shrugged off the rug he had put around her shoulders.

It had been a long time since she'd felt any reaction to a man. Jeremy had tried to reach out to her physically after Daisy's death. He had been grieving, too, and had needed solace and comfort. But she hadn't been emotionally equipped to give it to him. She had been too blind-sided by her own grief to give even a moment's thought to his needs. So he'd stopped trying and had let her push him away and it had been the beginning of the end.

She looked at David's beautiful long fingers, the nails clean and clipped short, the skin lightly tanned. She wondered what it would feel like to have them stroking other places. Touching, caressing, exploring. She shivered at the direction of her thoughts. For goodness' sake, the ink was hardly dry on her divorce papers.

But as the silence between them stretched, the need to just forget that day's unexpected whammy intensified. Forget about Ethel. Feel something other than the sadness. Feel alive deep inside instead of dead. Feel pleasure and desire instead of grief and loss.

The memory of their first kiss, months ago, in this very house returned. He had been patient and OK with crawling alongside her at her snail's pace but she had always known he desired her, wanted her. The thought was tantalisingly attractive and she heard her breath roughen and felt her lips part in anticipation.

David felt the change almost as soon as it happened. The silence between them became charged rather than companionable. He felt himself start to harden as her breathing stuttered and he felt the slight tremble of her hands. She looked directly at him, her eyes asking the question.

'David?' she said, her voice husky.

'No, Fran,' he said, his fingers stopping their caress. 'I don't think this is a good idea.'

'Please, David,' she whispered, 'kiss me. Help me feel something other than this horrible void.'

David felt his stomach lurch at her request. He shut his eyes. God knew, he wanted to. He sighed as he opened them again. Fran had moved closer, her face, her lips temptingly close.

'David,' she groaned.

He felt her warm breath on his face and when her lips pressed lightly against his he knew he didn't want to say no any more. Couldn't say no any more.

He opened his mouth and deepened the kiss.

Her little sigh of satisfaction went straight to his groin and he ached suddenly to be inside her.

Still he took it slow. He kissed her, long, slow, deep, explorative kisses as his fingers stroked her hair and her face and the back of her neck. They came to rest against her thighs as she opened her legs so he could position himself between them. He gently stroked the skin there, inching the material of her uniform slowly upwards.

Fran felt as if she was drowning in sensation. His kisses were making her hot and she didn't ever want him to stop. She pressed her lips against him harder, accepted his tongue into her mouth deeper. She wanted it all, everything he could give her. At last she was feeling something stronger, more potent than her grief.

His fingers as they stroked and swirled in gentle circles on her bare flesh were causing a tingling between her legs that she welcomed greedily. He was making her ready and she felt as if she would surely self-combust if he didn't touch her there soon.

He broke away from her lips and Fran mewed

her disappointment. 'Hush,' he whispered against her lips as he rose from his knees and gently pulled her upright with him, their bodies pressed intimately together. Fran felt his hardness pushing into her belly and the tingle between her legs intensified.

He stroked her face, pushing escaped tendrils of hair behind her ear, and gave her another slow, scorching kiss. She clung to his damp shirt, her knees almost buckling. Every time she thought she couldn't take another kiss without begging him to take her, his lips would move slowly, languidly against hers again and she wanted it go on for ever.

He broke away and stepped back slightly. He wanted to take it real slow. Make it easy and gentle, soothing to her battered soul. There would be plenty of time for frenzy. Right now, she needed a little tenderness.

Fran watched him through feverish eyes and wondered what he was doing. He was staring at her, his eyes roving over every inch of her body. She felt her nipples stiffen under his scrutiny and her breath catch at his blatant male appreciation.

He reached out and slowly undid the front zipper of her uniform. He used his two index fingers to push the dress up and off her shoulders and she shivered at his light touch on her skin. The garment fell to the floor and she stepped out of it.

She stayed very still as he walked slowly around her body, trailing his fingers around her middle as he went. She felt her abdominal muscles contract in turn as the fleeting touch of his fingers stimulated a response. He came back to stand in front of her and slowly knelt, pressing his face into her stomach and circling his arms around her, pulling her close.

Fran ran her fingers through his hair. He looked up at her and smiled. 'You are so beautiful,' he said in a low husky voice. He kissed her stomach and ran his tongue around her navel, dipping into it. She sucked in a harsh breath and her hand clenched a handful of his hair involuntarily.

He unclipped her bra and it fell down her arms. She tossed it away. He stroked the swell of her breasts with his long fingers, and smiled as her nipples stiffened beneath his touch. He raised himself higher and sucked one deep into his hot, wet mouth. Fran called his name out loud because it was so sweetly erotic she thought she was going to climax from that alone.

He rose slowly to his feet, releasing one breast and quickly claiming the other. Fran stretched her neck back and let her head loll as pleasure washed over her. He kissed his way up her neck, freeing her breasts from their sweet torture, and found her mouth again.

David thought he was going to explode at any second. Things were getting painfully tight in his trousers and he knew it was time to lay her in front of the fire and love her like she'd asked him to. He pulled away and felt a surge of pleasure at the drugged glaze to her eyes and her mournful 'No'.

'It's OK,' he whispered, and gave her another deep kiss. 'I'm just getting undressed.'

She nodded and swayed slightly as he let her go to do just that. He was very beautiful. His body was lean, his muscles nicely toned, perfectly delineated. He had the body of a distance athlete, the muscle fibres long and fine, not bulky like an iron-pumping gym junkie.

His erection stood out proudly and she liked it that he wasn't embarrassed by his nakedness or state of arousal. She put out her hand and traced the outline of his abdominal muscles and watched his erection twitch and bounce at each stroke of her fingers.

'Fran,' he growled in a low, deep voice, taking her hand and slowly lowering them to their knees. He kissed her, long and deep and slow, pushing her gently backwards until she was lying on the rug. He took a moment to look at her, the fire casting a warm orange glow across her pale skin.

He kissed her then—everywhere. Slowly and thoroughly.

And it was inevitable that the release that had been building slowly and surely since she'd first kissed him would arrive quickly and be all-consuming. As his hardness stretched and filled her and he ever so gently pulled out and re-entered, she orgasmed within seconds so intensely that it tipped him over the edge also.

They clung to each other as their bodies shuddered and surrendered to the flux of sensations. David could hear her crying out his name and he responded with hers, his face pressed into her neck as the last waves undulated through him.

Fran felt the damn walls burst as her climax broke over her. A jolt of intense pleasure swept through her, building and building until it erupted into a potent inferno of suppressed sexuality and sorrow. Every part of her was laid bare and in the moment of her most intense pleasure the floodgates to her grief were opened too and she wept.

She cried out in pleasure and pain, sobbing as she came down from the high. The tears that she hadn't allowed for Ethel earlier that day found their release. And tears also for Jeremy and Daisy and Jenny and all the things that were unfair in life. And for herself, too. Because, for a brief moment, she'd actually felt something other than her grief and it had felt wonderful.

CHAPTER SIX

DAVID DIDN'T MOVE but held Fran cocooned against him as her body heaved with the sobs that consumed her. Not even the crackling of the fire could be heard over her gut-wrenching cries. Her intense sexual release had obviously been the key to her built-up emotions.

He gently eased himself off her a while later when she moved under him, realising that he must be heavy on her slight frame. He gathered her close to his chest and stroked her hair as her sorrow slowly abated.

Fran took some deep breaths as the last of her tears dried up. She felt completely exhausted. Like she'd been put through a wringer. From the dizzy, intensely passionate heights of making love with David to the shock of her un-controllable outpouring of emotion.

Her head felt foggy and her bones felt heavy and her muscles ached with a weariness that went right down to a cellular level. With the rhythmic stroking of David's fingers through her hair, fatigue and post-coital malaise invaded her body with lassitude and she fell asleep to the reassuring thud of David's heart beating beneath her ear.

He knew the moment sleep claimed her. Her breathing changed from rapid and stuttering to slow and even. He reached his hand up behind him and felt blindly for the rug she had left discarded on the chair. He found the fringed edge and pulled it down, covering them both.

Even though it was spring, the nights could still be cool on the coast and as the heat from their joining dissipated they would no doubt cool off. Hopefully covering up would avoid the unpleasant experience of waking cold and shivering. The fire had burnt low and at some stage he would have to get up and tend it, but for now…he was pretty damn weary himself.

* * *

Dawn was poking its cold fingers into the room when David next woke. Fran hadn't moved a muscle and his arm was asleep from where her head had lain all night. He carefully extricated himself and pulled his underwear and shirt on for extra warmth, although he didn't do up the buttons. He crawled over to the fireplace on his hands and knees, stretching his joints as he went, cat-like. He was too old to sleep on the floor all night!

The fire was all but dead and he built another one. Fonzie stirred briefly and David gave him a scratch behind the ears before the puppy dozed off again. The fire burnt brightly and the radiant heat warmed him all over. He sat staring at the orange flames for a while, mesmerised by their beauty as he relived the beauty of making love to Fran.

He caught a movement in his peripheral vision and turned to see Fran sitting up. 'Hey, sleepyhead,' he said quietly, and smiled at her. She looked even more beautiful by the firelight. Her complexion looked warmer and her hair, dry now, looked like spun silk.

And there was an openness about her this morning, a frankness in the depth of her pale blue eyes. Like all her shutters and barriers had been removed and he was seeing the real Fran for the first time.

Fran smiled back at him and thought how homey and nice he looked by the firelight. Domesticated but in a way that was strangely sexy, too. His open shirt afforded her a view of his six-pack that she had touched last night and his cotton boxers fitted snugly.

She shuffled forward on her bottom, the rug pulled around her shoulders concealing her nakedness. She sat with her knees bent, her arms hugging her legs, her chin resting on her knees. He mimicked her pose and they sat opposite each other, the fire crackling beside them, just their toes touching.

'Are you OK?' he asked after they'd stared at each other for a few moments.

'No,' she said quietly, 'but I'm better than I've been in a long time.'

He nodded and they continued to stare at each other as the fire crackled.

'What happened with Jeremy?' he asked quietly after a while.

'He said he didn't love me any more and he left me,' she said.

David blinked at her frankness. His first instinct was to gather her up and make love to her again to help erase all the painful memories, but he sensed she was ready to unburden and he knew she needed that more.

'Why?' he asked.

'Because he blamed himself for our daughter's death.'

David felt the breath whoosh out of him. Hell! He didn't know what he'd been expecting, but it certainly hadn't been that. So Ethel had been right. 'Oh, Fran,' he whispered, because he was lost for anything else to say. He thought of Miranda and how close he'd come to losing her, and knew a fraction of Fran's pain. But she had known so much more grief than he had and it was no wonder she'd been so damaged when she'd arrived at Ashworth Bay.

Fran looked into the fire, away from the horror in his stare. 'Her name was Daisy. She died two years ago. She was ten.' She looked back at him then and she saw the light dawn. Had he done the maths and worked out that Miranda was the same age as her dead daughter would have been?

Of course! Now things made more sense. Knowing that Fran had had a daughter Mirry's age explained a lot of Fran's behaviour with Mirry over the past couple of months. Her initial reluctance to get too involved with his daughter and the almost pained expressions he'd sometimes witnessed when Fran had looked at Miranda.

'How?'

'She had a cerebral bleed from a ruptured AVM.'

Arteriovenous malformation. David sighed heavily and shuffled forward so her knees fitted between his and his thighs cradled hers. He rubbed his hands up and down her arms a few times and then rested them on her shoulders and kneaded them lightly.

He'd had a sixteen-year-old patient back when he'd first gone into general practise who had died as a result of an AVM. He'd been rushed to hospital after sustaining a head injury from crashing his motorbike, only to discover on CT that the rupturing of the AVM in his brain had come first and caused the accident rather than the accident being responsible for his head injury. He'd been dead before he'd even hit the ground.

Hell, most people didn't even know they had an AVM until it ruptured. There had even been a patient at the home a few years ago who had died at the age of eighty-three from an overdose and they'd made an incidental finding on autopsy of an AVM. He'd had the condition all his life and not known about or been killed by it.

David knew that an arteriovenous malformation was a congenital defect and that Fran probably had unreasonable levels of guilt about being responsible for Daisy having it in the first place. To that he could relate. Knowing he and Jen had passed HOCM on to Miranda had, and still did, give him terrible feelings of guilt.

It didn't matter that AVM was purely an accident of foetal development that caused a malformed area of blood vessels in the brain to have weakened walls, thus making them susceptible to rupture. Just as it didn't matter that he and Jen hadn't known about her HOCM until after Mirry had been born. The guilt you felt as a parent wasn't rational.

Fran's voice was husky as she continued. 'She came home from school one day and complained of a headache. I was at work.'

David saw the bitter twist to her lips and guessed she blamed herself about that also.

'Jeremy gave her some paracetamol and she said she might have a bit of a sleep. I got home about an hour later. Jeremy told me about Daisy and I went to check on her. I sat down next to her on the bed and noticed she'd vomited. I called her name and shook her but… she was unconscious…barely breathing.'

Fran closed her eyes against the pain that that day still engendered. It had been the worst day of her life. She felt David squeeze her shoulders and gave him a sad smile. 'She was rushed to hospital but it was too late, the bleed had been massive and the damage had been done. She was brain dead the next morning. We let her go that afternoon.'

A tear tracked down her cheek and glistened in the firelight. Fran swallowed the lump of emotion choking her throat. 'I left for work one morning and she'd stood at the front door waving me goodbye, and thirty-six hours later she was dead.' Fran's voice broke. 'If only I'd known that morning…. I wouldn't have gone to work or I would have given her twenty kisses goodbye instead of ten, I would have told her I loved her to the moon and back more than I ever had before.'

Fran stopped because she knew if she said

any more at the moment she was going to break down again.

'Oh, Fran,' said David, and pulled her into the circle of his arms, hugging her close. 'How awful. How very, very awful for you.'

Fran sheltered in the security of his arms and waited for the emotions to simmer down. She sat back after a while and turned her gaze back to the fire. 'I lost the plot after that. I could barely function. I spent whole days crying. I couldn't eat, I couldn't sleep. I quit my job. I existed within the four walls of our house and that was it. I was like a hermit.

'I pushed Jeremy away, too self-involved with my own grief and anger to respond to his. He blamed himself, hell, I'd blamed him in more than one argument and although, rationally, I didn't mean it, I think some small part of me did. Why didn't he check on her after she went to lie down? Why didn't he realise it was something worse than a headache? Daisy never had an afternoon nap. Why didn't he take her to the GP instead of giving her paracetamol?'

David listened to her quiet voice running back over that horrible day and the remorse and guilt since then.

'We became completely dysfunctional. I existed in this dark shell where there was just me and this constant oppressive grief. He would get up and go to work while I was sleeping and he'd came home late at night and we barely talked. And if we did, we argued. We were just going through the motions. Two people who were bound by a legal contract and a ring but emotionally disconnected from each other. I mean, something like this should have brought us closer, right?'

David shrugged as her questioning eyes sought his. 'A child's death is hard on relationships. Grief can make them go either way.'

She nodded and liked how his face looked with the firelight dancing shadows across his stubble. 'I know this sounds awful but by the time he told me he was having an affair and was leaving I was so removed from my old feelings for him that I didn't care. My grief over Daisy was still so huge that there was no room left for him and he was so needy all the time. He tried to reach me but I kept pushing him away until he decided not to come back one day. I just didn't have any love left for him.'

David bit back his automatic response to criticise Jeremy for his actions. He'd had an affair? Had he not realised that such a betrayal was the last thing Fran would have needed? 'Still,' he said gently, 'it was a pretty low act.'

She smiled at him for his words of defence and shook her head. 'No. I don't blame him for trying to find solace and comfort elsewhere. God knows, I wasn't there to give it to him but everyone in the family was in such a flap about it. All I cared about was that Daisy was gone. I couldn't understand it. My little girl, my baby, had been gone a year and still it hurt so much I could barely breathe. And they were worrying about the actions of a grown man.'

'It must have been a terrible time for everyone,' David said quietly.

She nodded. 'It was actually a relief, though,

you know, in lots of ways. I was so sick of the same old argument. About how he couldn't live with our decision and how could we have done that to our daughter. Like somehow it was easier for me because I wanted it more than he did.'

Fran drew in a ragged breath, remembering the horrible bitterness and recriminations that had been wreaked by their decision to donate Daisy's organs.

David stopped following Fran's meaning. What decision? The one to switch off Daisy's machines? Had Jeremy not grasped the full implications of Daisy's condition?

'I'm sorry? He had a hard time with the concept of brain death? He didn't want to withdraw treatment?'

Fran looked at him and shook her head. Their decision to donate Daisy's organs was still painful to think about, without having to talk aloud about it, but she was unburdening herself and suddenly she wanted him to know everything.

'No. We donated Daisy's organs. He was... reluctant.'

David felt his breath hitch in his throat. Fran had donated her daughter's organs? He searched her face for a sign that she knew the personal implications of this subject for him but found none. The Ibsens were showing discretion in their old age! If it wasn't for people like Fran and her courageous decision, children like Miranda died. His daughter had received the gift of a heart three years ago and without it she would be dead.

'It's such an awful time to be asked such an awful thing,' he said. How often had he thought about the family that had suffered so Miranda could live? Every day. At least.

Fran remembered that dreadful time vividly. The friction between Jeremy and herself over their decision to donate still felt as real as ever. 'You don't know the half of it,' she said, and couldn't block out the bitter tone shadowing her voice.

David looked at her assessingly. 'There was some conflict?' he probed gently.

She sighed. 'Jeremy was…unsure. It's funny

how life turns out, isn't it? Like a lot of people, I'd never really thought about what would happen in the situation we found ourselves in. But Daisy had. She'd come home from school only the week before and told me all about the discussion they'd had in class about the pros and cons of organ donation. She looked me in the eye and made me promise that if anything ever happened to her, I would donate everything they could use. I laughed and we did a pinkie promise.'

Fran paused and remembered vividly how she and Daisy had linked their little fingers together. Why wouldn't she have promised? It had obviously been very important to her daughter and, really, what had the chances been?

David didn't interrupt. He could see Fran had gone back in time and was reliving that day.

'But when we were actually faced with it, Jeremy was reluctant. And I got really mad. I cried hysterically and demanded that he fulfil our daughter's last wishes. I remember yelling at him, 'This is the only thing we can do for her now.' Fran shuddered. 'It was horrible. And we ended up haggling over her bits and pieces like…like we were fishmongers at a market.

'He drew the line at donating her corneas and no matter how much I tried to convince him that Daisy could give someone back their sight, he got really distressed at the thought of them removing her eyes….' Fran stifled a sob. 'Her beautiful blue eyes. And so I conceded and he consented to the rest.

'The whole year afterwards he had nightmares about Daisy. Maybe if I hadn't insisted on donating her organs, our marriage might have survived. But it was the one last thing I could do for her. I was her mother. I couldn't do anything else. Nothing.

'If I could have bought her back to life with my bare hands, I would have. If I could have gone back in time to that moment of her conception and fixed the broken link in the chain that gave her an AVM, I would have. If I could have traded my own life for hers, I would have done that also.

'But life's not like that and it didn't matter how much bargaining I did with any god I could think of, it was all futile and the only thing I could do for her was to see that her fervent wish be granted.

'Jeremy kept saying, 'She's only ten, what does she know? The teacher's just filled her head with fanciful stuff. She's not old enough to make an informed decision.' And I stood there in that room and begged him. 'I made a pinkie promise with her,' I said to him. I said it over and over. I told him I would end our marriage and never speak to him again. I called him gutless and callous….'

David gently wiped away the tears that were rolling down her face. He heard the raw anguish in her voice and it clawed at his gut. What a courageous woman Fran had been. He was seeing firsthand the flipside to Miranda's donated heart. Had the family who'd donated Mirry's heart been through this?

He had comforted himself with the fact that at least the anonymous family would be able to take solace out of their loved one's death and no doubt they had, but had their decision been as hard as Fran's? Did it still haunt them? Had it torn the family apart?

He hugged her close and marvelled that Fran had managed to survive the ordeal at all. He couldn't even begin to imagine how horrible it must have been.

She raised her head off his shoulder and looked at him with anguished eyes. 'I mean, did he really think it didn't tear me up inside, thinking about them cutting her open and using her for spare parts?' Fran sniffled and stared into the fire as she wiped her face on the rug.

'I've had more than my fair share of night-mares, too, but knowing Daisy has helped five people have a normal life again has given me enormous solace. If I was faced with that awful decision again, I wouldn't do it any differently.'

He stroked her cheek with the back of his hand and pulled her close. The room was bathed in full light now and Fonzie had gone out the cat flap to do his morning rituals.

Fran turned so she was leaning against him

now, her back to his chest, supported by the solid weight of his body. She felt weary from the emotional roller-coaster of the last few hours. Confession may have been good for the soul but it was totally exhausting for the body. David nuzzled her neck and they both let the fire mesmerise them for a while.

David watched the flames crackle in the hearth and tried to decide what was best. Would it help Fran to know about Mirry's heart transplant? Or would she run a mile? Maybe giving her a face to relate to would humanise her dreadful decision. Because the world needed selfless people like Fran and knowing that her decision had directly helped someone like Mirry might just be the soothing balm her damaged soul was craving.

There was only one way to find out for sure. 'You don't know about Miranda, do you? About her heart?'

'The Ibsens told me she'd been very sick and had to take medication for the rest of her life. I assumed when you told me abut Jen's HOCM that she's inherited her mother's condition and is being managed by medication.'

David shook his head. 'I wish,' he said ruefully. Talking about it had taken him right back to that fairly awful chapter of their own lives. Not the transplant itself but how sick Mirry had been and how he had despaired that she would die before she could undergo the lifesaving operation.

'She did inherit from Jen and was being managed pharmacologically, but three years ago her condition deteriorated very rapidly. Her anti-failure medication couldn't help her any longer and her options had run out. She needed a new heart. They emergency-listed her and we waited. It was awful. Waiting for someone else to die so Mirry could live.'

Fran heard the huskiness in his voice and felt his arms tighten around her.

'She was on the list for five days. I watched her deteriorate day by day. She got her heart on the sixth day.'

Miranda had had a heart transplant? She felt

her heart beat loud in her ears. She was too stunned to move. She said nothing, her mind a complete blank. Gradually her brain started to function again and things that had seemed odd fell into place.

Like Mirry's cat becoming the home mascot and David's insistence that Miranda always wash her hands after playing with Fonzie. Fran guessed that some of those daily meds Miranda took would suppress her immune system, making her more susceptible to infection and therefore requiring scrupulous hygiene around animals.

And Mirry's cute moon face. The steroids she'd be on were, no doubt, responsible for that as one of their side effects was the redistribution of fat, particularly around the face.

She turned in the circle of David's arms, grappling with the implications. 'So my daughter died two years ago and donated her organs. Your daughter received a heart from somebody a year before that. And we ended up living next door to each other.'

She stared at his face bathed in the gentle

glow from the fire and found it hard to wrap her head around what had happened. To be living next door to a girl who had benefited from the sort of loss that Fran had suffered felt like the last two years had come full circle. That the gut-wrenching decision and the self-doubt that had plagued her, particularly as her marriage had deteriorated, had all been worth it. There was enormous solace in knowing that someone just like Mirry had benefited from her heart-break. Suddenly Daisy's gift was personal instead of clinical.

Getting to know Mirry, watching her with the residents and Fonzie and being party to her exuberance and zest for life had taken the edge off the ache inside she still felt so keenly. And knowing this special girl as she did, what right did she have, did Jeremy have, to deny people like Mirry a normal functioning life? Deny David his daughter?

What if they hadn't consented? The thought that someone just like Mirry might have died because she'd let Jeremy sway her was unthinkable. Mirry suddenly embodied everyone who had received Daisy's organs. Not just her heart but her kidneys, her liver and her lungs. Fran knew with a sudden clarity that, after two years of uncertainty, she had made the right decision.

David nodded. He thought it was a pretty special coincidence. 'Pretty amazing, huh?'

Amazing or something more? 'Do you believe in karma?' she asked.

'Not really,' he admitted.

'Neither did I. Till now.'

David smiled and nodded. 'Maybe you're right. Maybe something out there orchestrated all this. Led you here so you could see firsthand how much your gift means to people like us and how it literally gives someone a chance at life. And so I could appreciate your sacrifice even more by seeing how much it cost you.'

He kissed her gently on the forehead and wiped the tear away that tracked down her cheek. 'Thank you, David,' she said, her voice husky.

'No,' he said, putting his finger under her chin

so he could look into her eyes. 'Thank you. I've often thought about Mirry's donor. We've written to them and the agency has passed the letter on but we've not had a response yet. It's frustrating because Mirry's really curious but I understand why now, more than I ever did.'

He sighed and picked up the poker and stoked the fire absently. 'You see, in my position it's easy to fool yourself into thinking that the decision to donate is cut and dried. Brain death is final and what's the point of wasting perfectly good organs, right? I think it's the only way you cope with the type of thoughts that you think while you're waiting and watching your daughter creep closer to death each day.

'There's a car accident on the news and someone's being airlifted to hospital with massive brain injuries. Or a pedestrian is rushed to hospital after collapsing from a suspected cerebral bleed. And all the time you're thinking. Have they talked about donation with their families? Are they on the donor register? Have they ticked yes on their driver's licence?

But listening to you...your decision was so courageous. Your determination to see your daughter's last wish granted in the face of such tragic circumstances and pressure from her father is truly amazing. You don't know how much your gift means to people like Mirry. People like me.'

'I do now,' she whispered. 'I really do now.'

Fran snuggled back into his chest again. They were both silent for a while, digesting everything that had happened.

'Where do we go from here?' asked David after a while. Her warm body pressed intimately against the length of his made him realise that the more recent revelations of the night had overshadowed the fact that they had actually made love.

A lot had happened in a very short space of time. He and Fran had shared an intensely intimate experience, she'd opened up and told him about her marriage and Daisy and they'd discovered a special link that was almost as compelling as their coupling.

Fran had mentioned karma and he was beginning to think she was right. He'd always felt a connection with her, from the day he had first met her on the beach and her sadness had resonated on a such a personal level for him. Maybe there was some kind of destiny at work and Fran had been meant to come to Ashworth Bay so they could heal each other. He did know one thing for sure. Having her here in his arms, being with her last night, was too right to be wrong or to let it go.

'I don't know if I'm up to any kind of commitment, David,' Fran said quietly. What they'd done last night had been amazing and everything that had happened since had been incredible, but it didn't miraculously remove her baggage or make her blind to the pitfalls of rushing into something. Things were going well. After two years of depression she'd never expected to feel so happy so quickly. She didn't think it wise to push her luck.

'I'm not asking for one, Fran. But I don't want to stop doing what we did last night. I won't crowd you, I promise, but I want to keep seeing you and getting to know you.'

It sounded nice to Fran and it had been a long time since nice had meant anything. She turned slightly so she was looking at him. 'Let's give it a try.'

David smiled against her lips as he claimed her mouth in a slow, sweet, triumphant kiss. When he pulled away they were both a little breathless.

'What about Miranda?' Fran asked. 'What do we tell her?'

David thought for a moment but knew what he had to say. Mirry adored Fran and it was tempting, knowing what he did now, to immerse his daughter in his happiness as well. The fact that Fran and Mirry could be good for each other also hadn't escaped him. Fran could help Mirry come to terms with the donation concept that he knew she grappled with. And Mirry could help Fran through her grieving as well.

But they were not good reasons to involve his daughter in a relationship that still had a lot of baggage to overcome. He'd made a vow to Jen's mother after Jen had died that he wouldn't expose Mirry to any relationships that weren't for keeps, and he felt as strongly about it now as he had then. And as significant as he felt this thing with Fran was going to be, he had to think of Miranda's needs.

'I think we should play it cool around Mirry, if that's OK with you. She's a young, impressionable girl who would dearly love to have a woman around and she's really taken to you. Until we know for sure that our relationship is going to be permanent, I'd rather stick with the we're-just-friends line around Mirry. I don't want to get her hopes up. I guess that goes for everyone, actually. If our relationship is common knowledge, it won't take Mirry long to find out at the home.'

Fran leaned in and kissed him. 'I think that's very wise, David,' she said, stroking her fingers over his chin and jaw enjoying the erotic feel of his stubble against her skin. 'How did you get so smart?' she said with a light teasing smile.

David was prevented from answering by a wet furball landing between them. Fonzie had obviously been frolicking in the dewy grass. He was cold and wet and Fran leapt up to depose a cold wet dog from her lap. The blanket didn't come with her.

David laughed and stared appreciatively up at her naked body. 'Hmm. Nice,' he murmured, rising from the floor with the rug and spreading it around her shoulders.

'Miranda's not due home till late this afternoon,' he said as he dragged her in close to his body. 'Fancy checking out my bedroom?'

'A bed? I thought you'd never ask! My back didn't appreciate the night in front of the fire.'

'Yeah, I guess our bodies aren't as young as they used to be.'

'Hey,' said Fran as they reached his bedroom door and shut a cold, wet Fonzie out. 'You speak for yourself.'

For the first time in two years she didn't feel ancient anymore. Despite what her back told her. And it felt good.

CHAPTER SEVEN

THE NEXT MONTH passed in the most wonderful daze for Fran. What cosmic forces had been at work to lead her to Ashworth Bay and her little cottage on the cliff she wasn't ready to analyse, she was just grateful. Suddenly, being drawn to the cottage from the minute she had seen it on the internet made sense—because it certainly hadn't at the time.

In fact, that she'd had such a strong gut feeling about the house had been very strange indeed. It had been a particularly dark time in her life. Her divorce had been looming and she'd reached the numb stage. Nothing had registered on her emotional radar at all. There had been no blips. She'd felt completely empty. Her mood flat. Blunted. The wild fluctuations in her emotions that had marked her earlier grief non-existent.

Yet on the day that she'd received her decree nisi, she'd seen the cottage and her gut had said, You must have this place, you belong in this cottage. Luckily she hadn't questioned it because, despite her barren emotional state, part of her had known that she needed a change or she was going to wither and die.

But looking back, maybe it had been about more than that. Maybe destiny or fate had been guiding her instincts and leading her to a place, to a family, that she needed, that needed her, before she could fully heal.

Her relationship with David blossomed and strengthened. She opened up and let him closer. Let Miranda closer. Sure, the events of the last two years still weighed heavily on her heart but they weren't the only thoughts that occupied her time anymore. Fran couldn't just see the light at the end of the tunnel—she could almost feel its warmth on her face.

The ache that she felt whenever she thought

about Daisy wasn't as acute. Being near Mirry and knowing about her transplant was helping Fran comes to terms with issues that had plagued her since her daughter's death. And having Miranda around made her realise how lucky she'd been to have had those ten years with Daisy instead of solely focussing on the two years without her.

They dined together most nights and every second weekend. When Mirry spent two days with her grandparents, Fran and David would spend the weekend in bed. They made love and they talked and they laughed and Fran was having fun. They ate…a lot. And Fran could see her body shape coming back, filling out, and how healthily her skin glowed now and how her eyes twinkled merrily.

Yep. Coming to Ashworth Bay had been the best decision she had ever made. She'd arrived four months ago a hollow shell desperately in need of a place to get her life back on track to feeling like part of the human race again. She was always going to have her past, she knew that, but she felt like her grief wasn't defining her anymore and that she could move forwards instead of staying in her destructive holding pattern.

And she had David to thank for that. David had been wonderful and gentle and had let her crawl along at her own pace, and Fran suspected she was falling in love with him. It was a scary prospect and she shied away from it. Love left you open to the potential for a whole lot of hurt and Fran had had enough hurt to last a lifetime.

Too much had happened over the past two years to be laying plans for the future. For now she was happy again and that was miracle enough.

After two years of blindly wandering in an emotional wilderness she'd known she had to make a change or go insane. But she'd never imagined that the move away from all she'd known and loved and all her history, both good and bad, would have been anywhere near this successful.

'Sister,' said Catherine frostily one morning, returning Fran's cheery greeting.

Fran gave her a big smile anyway. She'd

decided that she was going to wear the receptionist down with pure niceness. There was nothing
she could do about not being an Ashworth Bay
native but much she could do about becoming
one. She wasn't going anywhere!

Fran hummed her way through the morning
medication round. She'd managed to hasten the
process during her time at the home and could
do it in less than forty minutes if she had no
interruptions. If.

Polly, Molly and Dolly regarded her curiously
as she stopped the trolley outside their door.

'Happy today, dear?' said Molly.

'That's because it's a beautiful day,' said Fran,
putting the sisters' blood pressure medication
into plastic medicine cups.

'That it is,' agreed Polly.

'Are you sure that's all it is?' said the ever-
forthright Dolly.

This was just the kind of interruption Fran
tried to avoid. She smiled at them again and
feigned innocence before pushing on to the
next room. Subtle they weren't. She would

have to have been blind, deaf and stupid not to have noticed the Ibsen triplets' attempts at matchmaking.

Fran doubted it would be possible to dissuade them but refused to encourage them, either. What happened between her and David was evolving slowly and naturally and did not need any outside influence. She was happy with how things were at the moment and didn't want to give anyone false hope, least of all Mirry.

Especially when she wasn't sure exactly what she felt for David. He had been kind and gentle and they were close and becoming involved with him was fine, but she didn't want to think beyond that.

'Good morning, Ted. Good morning, Betty. Sleep well?'

'Like babies, Sister,' said Betty, and smiled serenely.

Fran raised her eyebrows at Betty and blinked as the elegant old lady gave her a wink.

'Do tell Dr Ross those little blue pills are marvellous next time you see him, will you, dear?'

Fran laughed as she heard Ted grumbling in the background about everyone in the home knowing their private business.

'What about you, Sister?' asked Betty. 'You look like you've found yourself a great sleeping pill, too.'

Fran's laughter petered out. Was it that obvious?

'Oh, don't worry, my girl. Your and Dr Ross's secret is safe with me.'

Later that afternoon Fran knocked on David's office door. He smiled at her when she entered and she felt her insides clench. Miranda was spending the next night— Saturday—at her grandmother's again and Fran knew that a fortnight of enforced abstinence and stolen kisses would make for a very passionate night indeed.

She crossed straight to the desk and he opened up his arms to her, pulling her down onto his lap. He kissed her thoroughly.

'Go and lock the door,' he whispered in her ear as he teased her earlobe with his teeth.

'No.' She laughed and kissed him instead.

'If you're going to keep kissing me like that you'd better lock it because I'm just about ready to sweep everything off my desk and have my wicked way with you.'

Fran chuckled. 'Patience is a virtue,' she said, and hopped off his lap and out of his reach. Distance was definitely called for at the moment and he was right—anyone could walk in on them.

'Betty knows about us.'

'Does she, now?' he said, stroking his chin absently.

'Oh, and she said to thank you for the little blue pills,' said Fran, grinning.

'Uh-huh! That's how she knows.'

'How?'

'Takes one sexually gratified woman to know another.'

'Oh, really? Well, frustrated is a better word at the moment,' she said, backing out of the room.

'One more sleep,' he said, and smiled as she blew him a kiss and left.

* * *

The next morning Miranda knocked on Fran's door.

'Hi,' said Fran, and stood aside so the child could enter. Giving Miranda free access to her home had happened so gradually and naturally it never occurred to Fran to do otherwise.

'Fonzie!' said Miranda, as the black puppy barked excitedly at their visitor and Miranda fell to her knees and patted him.

Fran watched them as they played. She'd just popped some raisin toast into the toaster. 'You had breakfast?' she asked Miranda.

'Not yet,' she said, picking Fonzie up and giving him a hug.

'Want some raisin toast?'

'Oh, yes, please. My favourite.'

Fran stopped in mid-buttering. It had been Daisy's favourite as well. She waited for the ache to come and the rush of painful memories, but found herself smiling at the anecdote instead.

Fran made Miranda wash her hands and

they ate together at the kitchen bench. Fran toasted another round, revelling in having her appetite back.

'We're having a picnic on the beach at lunch-time before I go to Granny's and I said to Dad that we should invite you and he said sure and so I'm here to invite you.'

Miranda had toast crumbs all over her mouth and Fran suppressed the motherly urge to pick up a cloth and wipe them away.

'Please, say yes, Fran. Fonzie can come, too.'

As if Fran could resist her bright eager face framed by those crazy red curls. 'What time?' she asked, and laughed at Mirry's triumphant squeal of delight.

Fran walked Fonzie down to the beach at midday. The sun was quite warm and Fran had smothered her fair skin with factor-thirty sun-screen and donned a wide-brimmed hat.

She found David and Miranda setting up under the shade of the trees that fringed the beach. Miranda ran off, chasing Fonzie up and down. She was wearing a long-sleeved sun shirt and also a hat.

David looked at Fran standing there, looking down at him. He couldn't believe how lucky he'd been. She looked stunning today in her denim cut-off shorts that just covered the tops of her thighs and a grey V-necked singlet shirt that bared the slightest hint of midriff.

Her feet were bare and her blond wispy hair was loose around her shoulders. She was so different from the woman he had first met on this beach those few short months ago. She looked fresh and relaxed and he wanted her. Now. Not tonight.

'No more sleeps,' she said, smiling down at him.

He grinned back and made room for her on the rug. They sat side by side, their arms and legs occasionally rubbing against each other's as they watched Miranda and Fonzie dash madly about. When they got tired of that, Mirry started to build a sand castle but was severely hampered by Fonzie's attempts to 'help'.

'I've got something to show you,' he said.

Fran's smile faded as she saw the serious look on his face as he handed her a folded piece of paper.

'I want you to read this and then I have something to ask you.'

Her hand trembled as she silently took it from him. She unfolded it and opened it gingerly, her eyes falling on David's familiar neat handwriting. It was a photocopied letter.

To the family who gave my little girl back her life.

As I sit and write this I find it hard to articulate my profound sorrow at your loss and the admiration I feel for you to have made such a selfless decision at the most devastating time in your lives. Words are completely inadequate to convey my gratitude to you. Because of your tragedy my daughter's life was saved.

She is doing incredibly well and I'm sure you could more than understand how much it means to have her back to her old self again. She has had a remarkably trouble-free post-op course and started back at school last week.

Please know that there's not a day that goes by that we don't think about you and your family and your wonderful gift to us. I hope that your decision to donate has given you some comfort in the midst of your sorrow. My daughter can talk and laugh and run again because of you and for that you have my eternal gratitude.

My deepest sympathies for your loss. My daughter would like to add something.

Daddy told me that your child died and gave me their heart. I know you must be very sad but you have made Daddy and I very happy. I promise to always take good care of my new heart. Every night as I go to sleep I will thank you and your child for saving my life.

Fran felt her eyes well with tears and she let them fall unchecked. She had received similar letters from all the recipients who had benefited from Daisy's gift. They were among her most prized possessions. Having a link with these anonymous people and hearing how much their lives had improved had been the one shining light in two years of darkness.

'That's beautiful, David,' she murmured. 'I'm sure it meant a lot to whoever received it.'

'I hope so. We've never received a reply so I can only assume.'

Fran heard his disappointment but her sympathies lay with the people who had gifted a heart to Miranda. She hadn't been able to answer her letters straight away, either. Receiving them had meant a lot but it had been many months before she'd felt strong enough to reply. 'It's not an easy thing to do, David. You may never hear back,' she said gently.

'I know. And that's fine, I understand that. But Mirry asks all the time if we've had a reply and I know she's disappointed that we haven't. She's only twelve, you know, but she's struggling with a concept that even a lot of adults find difficult to understand. The fact that somebody's child had to die so she could live affects her deeply. She has nightmares about it sometimes.'

Fran looked at the concern on his face. Not being able to help Mirry through this must be difficult for him. Parents were meant to have all the answers. 'So you want me to talk to her?'

David took her hand. He knew he was probably asking a lot. 'Would you? I don't want you to do anything that you feel you're not up to. I think maybe just telling her a little about Daisy will help humanise the transplant for her. I know Mirry's always wondering about her donor. I think it would help her to know what Daisy was like. It would make it more personal for her.'

The lap of the waves and the cries of the gulls faded as Fran's heart thudded loudly in her ears. Telling him about Daisy had been hard enough. Telling Miranda…?

David saw the indecision in her eyes. He kissed the palm of her hand. 'It's OK. There's no rush, Fran. Maybe it's something you could think about. If you're not OK with it yet, maybe you will be one day. There's no pressure here.'

Fran smiled at him, touched by his understanding. Once again he was giving her space and letting her set her own pace. 'Thank you.'

The three of them spent the next weekend together also. They went to Eumundi markets on Saturday, followed by a swim in the surf at Noosa, and the next day they went on a long bush walk, exploring the nearby Glass House mountains nature trails.

When they got back, Fran turned the oven down low and went to get out of her hiking clothes. Mirry and David were coming over for tea. She was cooking chicken Kiev, which was Mirry's favourite dish.

Her conversation with David on the beach came back to her as she showered. She'd been thinking about it all week. Maybe it was time to tell Mirry about Daisy after all. There was no denying how close she and Miranda were becoming or that Miranda enjoyed her company a lot. It seemed silly not to tell her all about her own little girl. Share a part of her life that would interest Mirry.

She wrapped a towel around herself and wandered into the bedroom. She opened her wardrobe and pulled out a box she hadn't unpacked. She reached in and grasped the first object that came to hand.

It was a framed school photo of Daisy taken not long before she'd died. Her ten-year-old face stared out at Fran and she found herself smiling at the cheeky grin and the crazy plaits that sprouted from her head, spider-like, as she traced Daisy's features with her finger.

The box was full of photographs and Fran knew that one day she'd be able to get them all out and display them, but for the moment just one would do. It was almost like the next step in her recovery. Keeping quiet about her past when it had hurt so much made sense but now, as the memories became joyful instead of sorrowful, it was time to show everyone that Daisy had existed. One photo at a time.

She dressed and placed the photo on a shelf of the television cabinet. Hopefully Miranda would notice it sooner or later and initiate a conversation. That would be the best way for it to happen. David was keen for her to talk with Miranda about the transplant but Fran would feel more comfortable if the impetus came from Mirry.

Fortunately, Miranda was very observant, and had been in the house less than ten minutes when she brought the framed photo into the kitchen where Fran and David were trying to be controlled and not touch each other lest they be sprung by a twelve-year-old!

'Fran? Who's this?'

David dragged his gaze away from Fran and how beautiful she was looking. He looked at the photo that Mirry held in her hand and realised immediately that it must be Daisy. The girl in the photo looked exactly like her mother and he felt his heart swell at how much Fran had lost.

David opened his mouth to tell Miranda to

put it back and not to touch stuff that didn't belong to her. Displaying her daughter's picture was a big step for Fran and he didn't want her regretting it because Mirry had acted impulsively. And a part of him was frightened that Fran might break like glass to see his alive-and-well daughter carrying around a picture of Daisy whose life had been so tragically taken away.

'It's Daisy,' said Fran, shooting David an it's-OK look. She waited for the pain and the over-whelming sense of loss to come, but it didn't. Instead, she remembered how Daisy had loved her spider-hair photo and how that particular hairstyle had taken her ages to complete.

'Who's Daisy?' Mirada asked, looking at the picture again.

'Daisy was my daughter. She died two years ago.'

Mirry gasped as she looked from the photo to Fran and back again. 'Oh, no, Fran!' she said, and tears welled in her eyes. She ran to Fran and threw her arms around her.

Fran felt tears dew her own eyes as she stroked Miranda's hair. David came around to where his two girls stood and sat beside them.

Miranda pulled away and looked at her father. 'Did you know, Daddy?'

'Yes, sweetie. Fran told me a little while ago,' he said gently, and put his hand on his daughter's shoulder.

Miranda looked up into Fran's face, her earnest gaze conveying a wealth of sorrow and sympathy. 'No wonder you were so sad that day on the beach. Was it cancer?'

Despite the solemn moment, Fran almost laughed out loud. It was such a grown-up thing to say and seemed so comical coming from a twelve-year-old.

Fran sat down on the chair next to David. 'No, she had something wrong with her brain and died very suddenly.'

'Was she brain dead?'

Fran sucked in a breath at Miranda's frankness. She had to remind herself that Miranda was no ordinary twelve-year-old. She had experience of things that most people never faced at any stage of their lives. And it did give her a good opening.

'Miranda,' said David gently, 'you shouldn't ask things like that.'

'No, it's OK,' said Fran, placing a hand on David's forearm. 'Yes, she was and, yes, we donated Daisy's organs. Five people are alive today because of her.'

Miranda looked at her with her earnest green eyes and looked back at the photo. 'I wish I knew what my donor was like,' she said wistfully.

'I'm sure the family will write you one day soon, sweetie. You just have to be patient. It's not an easy decision, Mirry. It can take a while to come to terms with.'

'Was it hard for you?'

'Yes, it was. But Daisy had a donor card and felt very strongly about donating her organs so that made it easier, and knowing that she saved someone just like you helps me every day.'

David squeezed her hand and Fran looked at him and smiled past the lump in her throat.

Miranda's finger traced Daisy's crazy hairdo. 'She has the coolest hair.'

Fran laughed. 'She hated her hair. She always wanted red hair, just like yours.'

'Really? What else was she like?'

'She was tall, like me, and quite athletic. A good little runner. She didn't like school much. She preferred being outdoors.' Fran laughed, thinking about Daisy's glum face as she had dragged her inside each morning and driven her to school.

'You don't seem sad anymore,' said Miranda.

Fran grinned. 'That's because you and your daddy have done such a great job of cheering me up. I still get sad but you've helped me with that a lot,' Fran said, and tapped Miranda on her cute button nose.

'I have?' Miranda's voice was full of wonder.

'Sure. Getting to know you has helped me realise that I had ten wonderful years with my little girl and that I should be concentrating on them. I've been sad for a long time about not having her any more but now I just want to be happy that I had her for as long as I did.'

Miranda nodded thoughtfully. 'Do you think that the child who donated my heart was like Daisy?'

Fran kissed her head. David was right. Mirry did have issues. 'Yup. I bet whoever it was, they were exactly like you and Daisy. Happy and carefree and outdoorsy and full of life and fun.' How did you answer that one? Fran couldn't be sure but if it gave Mirry a measure of comfort then it was worth it.

David listened to Fran set Mirry's mind at ease and he knew in that instant that he loved her and wanted to be with her for ever. The subject matter couldn't be easy for Fran but she was soldering on for Miranda's sake. For Miranda's peace of mind.

'Thank you,' he mouthed at Fran over the top of Miranda's head, and her answering smile caused his heart to fill with joy.

How much more time did she need? he

wondered. He knew without a doubt that he wanted to marry her. But even as those feelings swamped him, part of him urged caution. As far as Fran had come, he sensed it was still too early for such declarations.

'That was delicious,' David said, wiping the traces of chocolate sauce off his mouth with a serviette. He looked over Fran's shoulder, satisfied himself that Miranda was still engrossed in the TV and stole a brief passionate kiss. He licked the sweet stickiness from her lips and savoured it as he pulled away. 'Hmm. That was even more delicious.' He grinned.

Fran smiled back. 'I like an appreciative man,' she teased.

'Well, that's easy. You're a great cook.'

'It's nice to want to cook again,' Fran admitted.

David gave her a gentle smile and stroked the back of his hand down her cheek. He wanted to take her in his arms and kiss her again so the shadow that flitted through her eyes would be forgotten. But with Mirry in the next room, he couldn't really risk it. 'Come on,' he said, standing to remove himself from the temptation of her blue eyes and pink lips, 'I'll help you with the dishes.'

Fran washed. David dried.

'Thank you again, Fran…for before.'

'No problems. It felt good talking about her, actually. I'm pleased Miranda knows. Now if I'm ever a bit sad, she'll understand why.'

David threw caution to the wind, dropping his teatowel and backing Fran into the angle where the two kitchen benches met. He hoisted her up so she was sitting on the bench, pressed himself between her legs so her thighs were cradling his hips and gave her a long hard kiss. He felt himself grow tight as her mouth opened to his and knew he wasn't going to be able to sleep that night for thinking about this kiss.

'Miranda,' Fran warned against his lips as he pulled away slightly.

David drew in a ragged breath and placed his forehead against hers as he waited for his heart rate and breathing to return to normal. He pulled away and smiled at her. 'I'd better go,' he said, and helped Fran down off the bench.

Fran raised an eyebrow as the movement pressed him against her intimately and she could feel his readiness. She almost laughed at his pained expression and toyed with the idea of touching him there, even if it was only briefly. She shook her head—not fair.

'I'll get Mirry,' she said.

David moved away so she could pass and he watched her denim-clad butt sway out of sight. He pulled in a couple of deep breaths and gave himself a shake. He was a forty-two-year-old man, not a horny teenager!

Fran moved into the lounge, her limbs still heavy with desire. She spied Miranda asleep on the sofa and felt her heart melt at the sight. She squatted beside the couch and just stared at her beautiful moon face. Fonzie was dozing at Miranda's feet and she'd gone to sleep with her finger tangled in her curls.

Miranda stirred. Her eyes fluttered open and

she gave Fran a sleepy smile. 'Is it time to go?' she asked.

David entered the room. 'Goodness, Miranda Jane! Are you asleep? That's a first,' he teased.

'I felt tired.' She yawned and sat up, her red curls springing and settling into place around her head.

Fran felt a prickle of alarm at the base of her spine.

'Well, you have had a big weekend,' he said and ruffled her hair.

True, Fran thought. Two late nights and their bush walk today had been exhausting. She was a little tired herself.

'Say bye to Fran,' he said. 'School day tomorrow.'

Miranda gave Fran a hug and Fran held on for a bit longer than usual, enjoying the feel of Mirry in her arms.

'Thank you for telling me about Daisy. I wish I could have known her. It would be cool to have her living next door.'

Fran felt her breath hitch at the simplicity of the

picture Mirry had painted and allowed herself the luxury of indulging the fantasy for a second.

'Sorry,' said David quietly, apologising for his sleepy daughter's careless words.

Fran shook her head. 'It's OK,' she said sadly.

David blew her a kiss over the top of Miranda's head as they walked out the door.

It would have been cool, Fran thought as she shut the door. Way cool.

CHAPTER EIGHT

FRAN WAS HUMMING to herself as she walked into the nursing home the next morning. Not Catherine's stern 'Morning, Sister' or Reg's smelly leg ulcer dressing or cleaning up the mess caused by Gert's colostomy bag leaking managed to wipe the smile off Fran's face.

'Fran, every time I see you you're looking better and better,' commented Glenda at lunchtime. They were sitting with the residents, eating their lunch in the dining room, as they usually did. Glenda insisted that her staff eat with the residents to foster openness and communication. 'If I didn't know better, I'd say you were in love.'

Fran smiled at her and almost spilled the beans. Only the sudden quiet in the room as sixty residents paused in mid-mouthful and strained their ears stopped her. She looked around suspiciously and at least some had the good grace to look embarrassed.

Amazing! Most of the oldies were stone deaf if the cochlear destroying roar of the television was anything to go by, but give them a juicy piece of gossip in the midst of a noisy dining room and their hearing was as sharp as a newborn's.

Fran smiled at Glenda. 'Must be the sea air,' she said, and sixty pairs of knives and forks started clattering again. Fran laughed as Glenda winked at her.

At three o'clock Fran knew that Miranda wouldn't be far away and neither, for that matter, would her father! She was down at Reception, doing some photocopying much to Catherine's chagrin, when David walked through the door.

'Hey, there.' He smiled.

Fran looked up from her job and felt her insides wobble at that lazy grin. She smiled back at him and for a while they didn't do anything but stand and smile at each other, the glass petition separating them probably a good thing.

He was wearing a hot pink tie with lime green tigers all over it, and Fran didn't even notice.

'Honestly, Sister,' said Catherine with an annoyed eye roll, interrupting their moment, 'I can do this. It's my job, you're much too busy.'

Fran dragged her gaze away from David's sapphire eyes. 'I'm not doing anything and you're busy with the accounts.'

'Afternoon, Catherine,' said David, leaning on the counter and peering through the sliding glass window at them.

'Dr Ross,' Catherine acknowledged briefly.

The photocopier stopped in mid-job. Fran pushed a few buttons and looked at Catherine enquiringly. She could see David's amused face in her peripheral vision and she dared not look at him in case she laughed. Catherine was cranky enough at Fran invading her office.

'Here, let me,' bossed Catherine. 'Damn thing's been playing up lately. I usually just unplug and replug,' she said.

David winked at Fran as she moved out of Catherine's way. She was too ridiculously happy just to see him at the moment to pay any heed to Catherine's mood. Fran stood back, ignoring the receptionist's mutterings, and grinned at David instead.

As Catherine plugged the copier back in, the electrical sizzling and sparks didn't register either until Catherine's loud grunt cut into their silent flirting. It took Fran completely by surprise, as did the force at which the receptionist was thrown backwards across the office, landing on her back a good three metres from the photocopier.

Catherine had been electrocuted! Fran may have been slow during the incident but she sprang into action immediately.

'Catherine! Catherine!' she said, getting down on the floor, shaking the still receptionist vigorously and feeling for her carotid pulse. The ten seconds it took to assess the lack of pulse seemed like an age but there was no doubt in Fran's mind about the course of action required.

'Stand back,' she said to David, who had rushed into the office. Fran made her hand into a fist, raised it above her head and brought it down sharply, thumping Catherine hard in the middle of her chest.

David was kneeling beside them now. 'Well done,' he said as he felt for Catherine's carotid and it surged strongly against his fingers. Catherine moaned. 'You look like you've done that before.'

Fran let out the breath she'd been holding and realised she was shaking. Her whole body was reverberating to the loud bang of her heart. 'Once or twice,' she admitted, and helped David put Catherine into the recovery position.

'You keep monitoring her cardiac output and airway,' said David, rising and picking up the phone. 'I'll get Glenda to bring down the equipment and I'll call Phil to bring the ambulance.'

Glenda rushed down with the orange emergency box and the portable oxygen cylinder. They put the face mask that helped administer the oxygen on a protesting Catherine.

'Phil will be ten minutes,' said David.

'You want to put an IV in?' asked Fran, getting the equipment out of the box and assembling it.

'Why don't you? I figure anyone who can deliver a lifesaving pericardial thump is probably a pretty dab hand at IVs as well.'

'I am pretty good at it,' Fran said, and laughed.

Earl had heard the news and he rushed in as David was securing the cannula that Fran had inserted into Catherine's hand.

'Oh, my God! What's that for?' asked a panicked Earl.

'Just in case,' said David.

The office was even more crowded now with Earl's massive bulk and they made the decision to move Catherine outside into the foyer where there would be more room and there was better access for Phil when he arrived. David gave Earl a job of finding a pillow and blanket because his fussing was adding an extra level of stress to the situation that none of them needed.

Catherine moaned again and David spoke to her quietly. 'It's OK, Catherine. You were electrocuted but you've been very lucky indeed. Fran was very quick off the mark and saved your life. We're getting you to hospital so you can be properly checked out.'

David squeezed the starchy receptionist's hand as she nodded weakly at him. She appeared OK now but she had been in contact with enough electricity to stop her heart. He knew the hospital would want to do at least twenty-four hours of cardiac monitoring.

Fran inspected the small wound on Catherine's hand where she'd been holding the electrical plug. It was about the size and shape of a five-cent piece but it was white in the middle with a dull blackish grey outer ring.

'Deep thickness?' she asked David quietly.

He nodded at her. It would probably need a skin graft. Luckily it was a small area.

'Fran, I know you're busy but Sid's not looking too good. Do you think you could take a look?' said Molly, entering the fray and then realising something serious was going down. 'Oh, my,' she said, patting her chest.

'You go,' said David, 'Phil can't be that far away.'

Fran got up from the floor and followed Molly. Sid met them halfway along the corridor. 'Oh, there you are, Fran,' he said. 'I'm feeling right terrible. The pain is the worst it's ever been.'

Fran didn't need one piece of medical technology to realise the truth of Sid's words. He looked grey and was sweating. She touched his wrist and his skin was cool and his rapid pulse fluttered weakly against her fingers.

'I think I'm going to be sick,' he said.

Sid promptly vomited. All over Fran. It poured out in one smooth red fountainous stream. Fran gasped at the shock and looked down at her soiled uniform. Thank God they no longer wore white. The smell of warm regurgitated stomach contents filled her nostrils and she suppressed the urge to gag herself.

She ignored the grossness of wearing somebody else's bodily fluids and concentrated on what was important. The vomit was red. Not dark and grainy like coffee-grounds, which would have indicated an old bleed, but bright red and heavily metallic, indicating a fresh bleed. And a big one at that.

'I'm so sorry, Fran,' groaned Sid as he doubled over and clutched his stomach.

'Occupational hazard, Sid, don't worry about it. Come on, now,' she ordered, taking his hand and dragging him back around to where David—and hopefully an ambulance—would now be waiting. Please, let Sid make it without passing out, she thought.

'Another oxygen mask, Glenda,' said Fran, as she rounded the corner.

David, Glenda and Phil all looked up from their ministrations on Catherine.

'Put him on the stretcher,' said David recovering first from the sight of a bloodied Fran, who looked like she'd been stabbed.

The stretcher was just inside the door and Fran led Sid straight to it.

'Might be a bit longer, Catherine,' said David, and indicated to Glenda to take over from him so he could attend to Sid.

'I'm fine, Dr Ross,' she said firmly.

'You want to get changed?' he asked Fran, handing her a cannula and a tourniquet.

'After,' Fran dismissed ignoring the cloying metallic smell and the cold wet feeling against her skin. She took the equipment and concentrated on finding a vein instead.

David shot her a grateful smile. He wouldn't have blamed her if she'd insisted on changing and showering immediately. But Fran was nothing if not professional and obviously knew a serious situation when she saw one. Two hands were going to be better than one if they had a hope of saving Sid.

'You got some plasma expander in the ambulance?' David asked Phil as he found a vein in the crook of Sid's elbow and slid a wide-bore cannula into it.

Phil had two flasks and as soon as Fran had cannulated her side she helped Phil attach giving sets and hook them into the waiting IVs.

David applied some oxygen and Phil pulled the knob on the stretcher that allowed him to raise the end of the bed to help with Sid's shocked status. Fran took a quick BP. Seventy systolic—not good.

Miranda chose that moment to walk through the doors and she gasped when she saw Fran, who looked like she'd been in a war zone.

'It's OK, sweetie,' Fran smiled. 'It's not mine.'

'We're a little busy, Mirry,' said David, wanting his daughter to be spared the gruesome sight of Sid bleeding out in the foyer of the nursing home. 'Go with Molly to the kitchen and get something to eat. Start your homework. We're nearly done here.'

Miranda looked pale and frightened and looked behind her doubtfully as Molly ushered her away. David exchanged a look with Fran. He could see he would have some explaining to do when he got home that night.

'How much do you reckon he's lost?' asked Fran, as she watched David palpate Sid's abdomen. It was tense and rigid.

'Hard to say. What was his BP?'

'Seventy.'

David looked at Fran and didn't say any more. He just kept working, prioritising, because if he didn't keep doing something he would shake the silly old fool for refusing treatment. This was exactly what Sid had been told would happen.

'Let's load them and go,' he said to Phil.

'What about air evac?' asked Fran.

'By the time it's organised we can have him in Nambour. Can you come, too?'

'I suppose.' She looked at Glenda, who nodded.

'It's easier with two patients, especially with one as critical as Sid.'

'What about Miranda?' she asked.

David smiled at Fran, getting a real kick out of her concern for Mirry. It was nice to know that, with everything else that was happening, his daughter was at the top of her priorities.

'We'll look after her,' Glenda assured him.

They loaded their two patients into the ambulance. Luckily, this model was equipped with two stretchers, as were all remote-area vehicles. Phil radioed ahead and they were driving speedily through the streets of Ashworth Bay before Fran could blink.

Sid was as stable as they could make him so it was a matter of getting to the nearest hospital as soon as possible and hope like hell the bleeding had stopped or slowed or, if not, that they were replacing Sid's lost blood quick enough.

Both Sid and Catherine were attached to cardiac monitors and Fran and David kept watchful eyes on the traces. Due to the electrocution affecting the conduction system of her heart, Catherine was more susceptible to lethal arrhythmia, and for Sid, one of the signs of worsening blood loss would be myocardial ischaemia and that would show up very quickly on his ECG trace.

Fran had forgotten how nauseating it was to be sitting in the back of an ambulance being dragged backwards at high speed. The cars were quite tall with a high centre of gravity, which made them sway sickeningly. That, combined with the dark bloody stain drying on her uniform, was not good for her stomach.

'You OK?' David asked, squeezing her hand.

'Nothing that a shower and a sedate sixty won't fix.' She smiled.

David looked at her and thought she'd never looked more beautiful. Fine blond tendrils of hair had escaped her plait and wisped around her face, her lipstick had smudged off and she was covered in Sid's stomach contents. But she had ignored her own discomfort and not only saved one life today but hopefully two. And she had been kind to Mirry and worried about his daughter before she'd even thought about herself.

He knew it was the wrong time and the wrong place and she might not be ready to hear it yet, but he didn't want to live another minute without telling her.

'You look beautiful and I love you, and I know this isn't the most romantic setting and I don't even have a ring, but I want to marry you. I know you're not ready yet, I just want you to know.'

Fran didn't move. Then she blinked. And blinked again. David had spoken aloud the words she hadn't even been game to think. She waited for the pain to come, for the grief, for the absurd laughter, and for a rejection to form and come out her mouth. But it didn't. A notion that had seemed unattainable just a few short months ago suddenly seemed feasible. She and David and Miranda, living together. He loved her.

'Say something.'

Fran opened her mouth to speak and then shut it again. She waited a few seconds. 'I'm…I'm.'

Sid's monitor alarm went off and they both startled. David gave himself a shake as he checked his patient. A lead had come loose and was causing interference. He sat back down next to Fran. This definitely wasn't the time for it. He needed to focus on Sid and Catherine. But he hadn't been able to stop himself.

'I'm sorry,' he apologised. 'I shouldn't have brought this up now. Lets talk abut it later, OK?'

Fran nodded her head because she wasn't sure what she'd been going to say or even how she felt. All she knew was that David loved her, and hearing those words had made her feel good, not bad. Calm, not panicked.

They watched the monitor traces for a while in silence.

'What are his chances?' Fran asked quietly.

'Slim,' said David, and he gave her a grim look.

'David, it's not your fault. You tried to get him treatment.'

'I know, I know. It's just such an unnecessary emergency.'

Fran nodded. 'You can only do so much, David.'

Phil pulled up in the ambulance bay at Nambour General soon after. Fran was grateful to be stationary for the few seconds it took for Phil to open the doors and then it was go, go, go. Rush, hurry, hurry.

Fran, who was at home in an emergency department, stood back and let the Nambour team take over. David was in the thick of it and she was happy to let them go for it—she needed a shower desperately. The triage nurse gave her some towels, a pair of theatre scrubs and pointed her towards the staff showers.

Ten minutes later she was done. She deliberately forced herself not to think about what had transpired in the ambulance. She knew Phil would want to get back to Ashworth Bay and there was Mirry to think about so she didn't linger.

It felt great to be clean and smell good, and David whistled as she approached and she felt like a million dollars. Like some kind of super-model instead of plain squeaky-clean Fran.

'Come on, let's go home,' said David, giving her a brief hug, and Fran almost cried it sounded so good.

Fran quickly ducked her head in to say goodbye to Catherine. She was sleeping so Fran squeezed her bandaged hand and whispered, 'Take care, Catherine.'

The receptionist's eyes fluttered open and her lips allowed a fleeting smile. 'Thank you, Fran. I owe you my life.'

'Catherine?' said Fran, unable to believe her ears. 'Did you just call me Fran? I thought I had to be a native for fifty years before you'd call me by my first name.'

'I always make exceptions for outsiders who save my life.' She smiled.

Fran laughed. 'If I'd have known that, I would have photocopied long ago!'

Catherine laughed, too, and Fran felt she'd glimpsed the doll that Glenda had insisted Catherine was once you got to know her. It felt good, leaving on such a high note.

They rode up front with Phil on the return trip and he chatted away amiably to them. The more sedate pace had them back in Ashworth Bay in half an hour instead of the fifteen minutes it had taken the other way, and Fran's stomach was grateful. Phil dropped them back at the home and Fran couldn't believe it had only been two hours ago that Catherine had been electrocuted and the afternoon had gone to hell in a hurry.

They found Mirry asleep in the television lounge between Molly, Dolly and Polly.

David frowned. Asleep again before bedtime? That just wasn't like his Mirry. He felt a prickle of alarm and quashed it immediately. Panic was stupid. He was a doctor. Assess her first.

'Come on, darling,' he said, kissing his daughter lightly on the cheek. Her face was flushed and felt hot against his lips. 'Mirry?'

She stirred and opened her eyes. 'I don't feel very well, Daddy. I'm so tired,' she said, and shut her eyes again.

David sat her up, concerned that her breathing sounded noisy. He listened to her chest with his ever-present stethoscope and heard the tell-tale fine crackling sound of fluid in her airways. He inspected her hands and noticed they looked a little puffy.

David tried to quell the sickening rise of dread inside. He tried not to think about how tired Jen had been before she'd died or how tired Mirry had always been before her transplant.

'What is it?' asked Fran. 'What's wrong?' She could tell by the look on David's face he was worried. Hell, he looked worse than worried. He looked petrified.

'We need to get her to Brisbane. Right away,' he said, sweeping Miranda up into his arms. 'Will you come?'

And right then and there, it hit her. As he stood in front of her, the worries of the world on his shoulders, asking her to be with him, she knew she couldn't refuse him. Because she loved him. She loved David Ross and she wouldn't deny him in his hour of deepest need.

Even though as she followed him, a very sick Miranda lolling in his arms, a dreadful sense of *déjà vu* settled around her. She loved him but she couldn't watch another child die.

CHAPTER NINE

THEY MADE a quick detour home. David threw clothes and toiletries for him and Miranda into a bag. Fran got out of the scrubs and packed a small overnight bag. She grabbed a book off the bookshelf and tossed it in, too. They were gone again ten minutes later.

Fran offered to sit in the back with Miranda and as much as David wanted to have her close to him, to gain reassurance from being able to touch her, he knew an excellent suggestion when he heard one. Fran could keep a close eye on her and alert him to any worsening of her condition.

Miranda flopped her head against Fran's arm as Fran buckled herself into the middle seat. She put her arm around the girl's shoulders and cradled her carefully. She felt so hot and Fran didn't have to feel Miranda's pulse to count it—her little body shook with each bounding thud.

Fran watched David's grim profile as he sped through the night, cursing people who drove too slowly and only really relaxing a little once they hit the dual carriageway that would take them straight into the heart of Brisbane.

What a day! Fran would never have thought it could have got any worse after delivering an electrocution and an acutely bleeding critical patient to Nambour. Surely that had been a reasonable assumption. But this? This had come from left field and Fran refused to let her mind wander down the what-if track.

But despite that, the sense of *déjà vu* got stronger and stronger as they neared their destination, and the sick feeling she had felt two years ago as she had ridden in the ambulance with Daisy returned and refused to be quelled.

David seriously doubted he'd get to the Children's Cardiac Hospital in Brisbane without being nabbed by a speed camera. His powerful car ate up the distance and while he wasn't driving recklessly it was a machine that could handle speed effortlessly.

He just had to get her to hospital as soon as possible. He'd pay a hundred speeding fines if necessary as long as Mirry was in the best place she could be. In Brisbane at the hospital where she'd had her transplant. Where he took her for her regular outpatient appointments. Where there was specialist medical attention.

As he drove he tried to be calm and rational. He was a doctor, for goodness' sake, even though he was suddenly struck with amnesia about anything medical. His worry and fear were rendering him totally useless! Stop it, damn it! Think man, think!

Clarity finally came to him and he felt less fearful when he could think like a doctor instead of a father. It was probably just a bit of a chest infection that had taken hold. She'd been tired for a couple of days and he'd noticed an occasional dry cough. A chest infection would explain the fine crackles he'd heard on auscultation of her chest also.

He clung to that as he drove because the alternative was too awful to contemplate. Rejection. Even thinking the word sent a chill down his spine. They had been very lucky so far. Miranda had had a very good post-operative course, free from the complications that a lot of patients suffered.

No episodes of rejection. No signs of coronary artery disease. But that didn't mean she was going to avoid them indefinitely. Knowing rationally that rejection was at its most common in the first year post-transplant didn't help when he also knew it could strike at any time.

David was also aware that most cardiac transplant patients required several transplants over the course of their lives—particularly paediatric patients, due to their size and growing bodies. He'd been prepared for the eventuality but had hoped that they would buck the trend or at least set the record for the longest transplanted donor heart.

David had adjusted the rear-view mirror into

a position where he could see Miranda's face and he checked it frequently. He could also see Fran's face and the worry etched between her brows. He realised suddenly that this must be hard for Fran. It must seem eerily familiar and he cursed himself that he'd been selfishly thinking of only himself when he had asked her to come with him.

He glanced back as the car glided to a halt at the first traffic light on the highway. Having to stop was frustrating, but at least he knew they were nearly there.

'How's she doing?' he asked.

'No change. Still sleeping,' said Fran. He looked desolate and Fran knew better than anyone how that felt. She touched his shoulder with her spare hand and gave it a squeeze.

David placed his hand over hers and gave her a sad smile. 'Thank you for being here. I know this can't be easy for you.'

Fran felt a lump rise in her throat and tears well in her eyes. She nodded, too emotional to speak.

Eight minutes later they were pulling up in

the emergency parking bays of the hospital and David rushed Miranda inside. When Fran joined them a few minutes later she found a pale Miranda lying on a narrow trolley, hooked up to a cardiac monitor, nasal prongs delivering a trickle of oxygen, a doctor listening to her chest and a nurse taking blood.

'Just a scratch, darling,' said the nurse, whose name tag announced him as John, as he pierced her skin with the needle. Miranda didn't even murmur. Fran sat next to David and he took her hand and held on tight. The doctor examining Miranda took the stethoscope out of her ears.

'Well, what do you think?' asked David, standing. Fran stood with him.

The woman approached. She looked to be in her late forties. She was tall and thin and wore glasses with crazy rainbow frames. She had friendly eyes and the photo on her name tag had a sticker of Shrek stuck over the top.

'I'm Anne Cahill,' she said, and held out her hand to Fran.

'I'm sorry,' said David, rubbing his hands

through his hair. 'This is Fran. Fran, Anne is the cardiac surgeon who did Miranda's transplant.'

Fran shook the woman's hand and felt reassured by her firm grip. She seemed confident and competent.

Anne ushered them to the chairs. "I'm pretty sure you're right, David. I think it's just an opportunistic chest infection that's taken advantage of Miranda's suppressed immune system. But I want some bloods, a chest X-ray, a sputum sample and an echo before I make any definitive diagnosis. Let's get that all organised first and then we'll talk again. OK?'

David nodded and tried not to look miserable. Miranda looked so still. It was hard to feel reassured when his little dynamo, his whirly-gig, his bundle of energy was lying so motionless. As a doctor he had to think of all the possibilities, including the worst-case scenario, and he knew Anne Cahill well enough to know that rejection was at the back of her mind, too. As a father the only scenario playing in his mind was the worst.

Fran and David sat together listening to the rapid blip of the monitor indicating Miranda's heartbeat as activity went on all around them. John came in and hooked up some IV fluids to the cannula he'd left in Miranda's arm when he had taken blood earlier. The portable X-ray machine was wheeled in and two films were taken of her chest from different views.

Anne came back in with the heavy, portable echo-cardiogram machine and perched herself on the trolley beside Miranda. It was similar to an ultrasound machine used for foetal sonography but was specifically designed to view the heart. The transducer was similar and the gel she squeezed onto Miranda's chest to improve the view was also the same.

She asked John to turn the overhead lights off and Fran and David watched the screen as an image of Miranda's heart came onto the screen.

Anne gave them a running commentary as she manipulated the transducer through the gel, angling it different ways to achieve the best view. 'No enlargement or oedema of the walls....

Good blood flow…. No regurg…. No growths on the valve leaflets…. Good left ventricular function…. Ejection fraction…fifty-nine per cent…. Could be better but not too bad….'

David shut his eyes. Fifty-nine? On her last echo the ejection fraction had been sixty-seven. Still, Anne was right, it could be much worse. Pre-transplant it had been twelve per cent!

Anne finished up and wiped the goo off Miranda's chest. Miranda's eyes fluttered open. 'Hey, there, poppet,' Anne crooned. 'Not feeling so good?'

David squeezed his daughter's hand and kissed her forehead, greatly relieved to see that the IV fluids were rallying her a little.

'Hi, Dr Anne,' said Miranda in a very small voice. 'I'm tired and it hurts to cough.'

'We're going to fix that, I promise.' Anne smiled.

Miranda nodded and drifted back to sleep.

'We're getting her to the ward and I'm starting her on some broad-spectrum antibiotics until we know what we're dealing with.

I'll talk to you upstairs some more when the blood results come back.'

David nodded. He knew that Anne wanted to be in possession of all the facts before she spoke to him—he'd want to if the positions were reversed. For the moment Miranda seemed OK and was in the best place possible. He looked at Fran and she smiled reassuringly. And Fran was here, too. He just had to try and stay positive.

They were moved to the ward shortly after and David and Miranda were greeted enthusiastically by the staff. It was no cliché to David to describe them as family. The many familiar faces had seen them both through thick and thin and the entire medical team had always treated them like one of their own.

Fran sat beside Mirry's bed and watched her chest rise and fall and her rib cage reverberate with each pound of her heart. David paced around the room, then prowled up and down the corridor and then came back and paced some more. Mirry had a bit of colour in her cheeks now and Fran was relieved by Anne's prediction that it was probably just a chest infection.

Last time she had sat beside a young girl's hospital bed the news had been very grim. She knew David was concerned but, comparatively, this was good news. Surely he could see that? He seemed very worried still and Fran wondered if there was something he wasn't telling her.

He smiled at her every time he re-entered the room and seemed pleased that she was there. She wanted to say something to ease his torture but she knew how trite words were in these situations. Hopefully her quiet presence was enough.

Anne entered the room, took one look at David and said, 'You look awful.'

'I feel awful.'

'I just came to say that there's been a hiccup at the lab and the tests, all the hospital's blood tests, have been delayed. But I can see we need to talk. Come on, you know the way.'

Anne left the room and David turned to Fran.

He wanted to have this talk but he was frightened of what he would hear. He needed Fran by his side. 'Come with me? Please?'

Fran nodded. David needed her and she loved him. How bad could the news be?

'OK, to recap,' said Anne, once they were sitting in a small cosy room on deep comfortable chairs. David held Fran's hand and she stroked his reassuringly.

'I think all this is is a chest infection. Because of Mirry's immunosuppression, it's taken a real hold. She has a fever and her X-ray shows pulmonary congestion. I'm going to treat her with the antibiotics and some medication for her ejection fraction. I think the chest infection is playing havoc with her lungs, which is in turn causing right-sided congestion.'

She stopped to see that Fran and David were taking it in and they both nodded at her.

'Now the other possibility, and we'll know for sure when the tests come back, is rejection.'

David felt a hot fist slam into his chest. The

word had been mentioned out loud and he was being forced to confront it for the first time.

Rejection? Fran sat a little straighter. Rejection? She hadn't even thought about that.

Anne held her hand up. 'I don't believe it is for a moment. I only mention it because I know you're driving yourself crazy, David Ross.'

'Her symptoms could also indicate rejection.'

She looked at him. They could? Fran didn't know enough about transplant medicine to decide.

'Yes, they could.'

'So what happens if it's that?'

'It's not. Her echo is good.'

'What if it is?' David insisted. Why, he didn't know. He knew what would happen if it was. He just needed to hear it from her mouth.

'We'd need a biopsy to confirm and then try her on different anti-rejection medication.'

'And if that didn't work?'

'David,' said Anne gently, 'stop this. This is pointless. It's not rejection.'

Miranda could be rejecting her heart? Fran

started to feel the darkness claim her again. She was going to have to watch another little girl die. She couldn't. She just couldn't.

'What, then?' David demanded. He knew Anne was right but he just had to hear the worst-case scenario.

'She'd need to be relisted.'

David sagged back in the chair, his worst fears realised. Fran looked at the utter desolation on his face.

'I don't think I can go there again, Anne,' he said quietly.

'David…the bloods are going to come back with a raised white cell count. Her sputum will grow a bug. We're going to treat Mirry with antibiotics and you can take her back home.'

'Of course,' he said, giving himself a shake. Now he'd confronted the worst, he needed to concentrate on the most probable. 'I'm sorry, Anne, I just needed to know it all.'

She nodded and smiled. 'I'll come and find you as soon as I have the results—I promise.'

Anne rose and left and David felt immeasurably better for reasons he couldn't explain. It was as if by confronting his worst fear, acknowledging it and plotting a course of action to combat, it had taken the power out of his fear. And Anne's certainty that Mirry wasn't rejecting her heart bolstered his confidence.

He turned to Fran and was surprised to see tears tracking down her cheeks. 'Fran?' She didn't answer him. She just sat there, very still, staring at the floor, her hands gripping the arms of the chair, her knuckles white. 'Fran?' he said again.

She could hear him calling her. Somewhere through the fog of jumbled thoughts and emotions and the thunder of her heart echoing in her ears she could hear his voice. But the voice saying *Get out, run away, you can't do this again* was louder. It wasn't until his third try that she was able to pull herself out of the escalating panic settling around her and engage her mouth.

'I can't do this. I have to go.' She got up, put her bag over her shoulder and walked out of the room.

David sat staring after her for a few seconds.

Had he asked too much of her? Probably, but, damn it all, she'd been through this kind of thing before and knew how frightening and worrying it was. Was it asking too much for her to just be there for him?

And what about Miranda? His daughter adored her. Even if it was just a chest infection, with Mirry's immunosuppressed state she was sicker and would take longer to bounce back. Fran had become such a fixture in Miranda's life and the little girl worshipped the ground Fran walked on. And if the worst happened? If it was rejection? Mirry would have enough to cope with without the confusion of Fran deserting her.

David felt his worry and frustration mix into a potent brew. His desperate need to have Fran by his side sparked his legs into action and he was out the door and following her down the corridor. He caught up with her as she got into the lift and he managed to get his hand between the two doors before they slid shut.

Fran looked terrible. Her pale blue eyes

looked like they had the day he'd first met her on the beach. Empty. Void. It was only the reddened rims, the muted sobs and the stream of tears that showed him her anguish.

'Please, don't leave,' he said quietly as the lift took them downwards. He heard a gurgling in her throat and she started to sob louder. 'I know this must be really hard for you and I'm being selfish because I love you and I'm scared for Mirry and I need you. And Mirry needs you, too. She loves you as well. Don't desert her in her hour of greatest need. Don't desert us.'

He put out his arms to hug her but Fran shook her head and took a step back. She was crying hard now, her face completely crumpled as tears fell unchecked and her distressed sobs echoed loudly in the lift. Her nose was running and mixing with her tears and she knew she must look a complete wreck but she didn't care.

'How…long,' she fumbled between hiccupy sobs, 'have you known…about the poss-possibility…of rejection?'

The lift pinged and she stalked out. David followed.

'I was worried about it the minute I listened to her chest and heard how wet it was,' he said, following her out the sliding entrance doors into the warm night.

So he had known of the possibility hours ago. Why hadn't he said anything? Fran had been out of nursing too long and didn't know enough about the transplant specialty to have thought about the awful possibility. If he had used the R-word back in Ashworth Bay she would never have come. She kicked on some more speed. She had to get away from there.

'Where are you going?' he asked as she charged on.

'Taxi rank,' she choked out around her sobs.

David caught up with her and gently pulled on her shoulder until she spun around to face him. 'Fran, if you must go, take my car.' He fished in his pocket for the keys. 'I won't be needing it for a while.'

She reached for his keys but he pulled them

away. 'Not until we talk.' They were standing in a grassy area at the front of the hospital. It was away from the main lighting and reasonably private.

Fran's initial crying had waned a little, leaving her with a few dying sniffly sobs. 'Forget it. I'll get a taxi,' she said. Fran didn't want to talk. Yes, she was running away. She knew that. But the alternative was too much to bear.

She'd sat and watched her daughter die two years ago and the possibility that this was the beginning of the end for Miranda was too painful to bear.

'Fran, please!' said David, catching her and stopping her progress again. He was starting to feel frantic. He knew this was about more than Mirry being sick but he'd be damned if he'd let the best thing that had happened in his life walk away without fighting for her.

'I can't make you stay. I can't make you love us. But I can ask you to give me one good reason why you're walking away when we need you most. You owe me that at least.'

Fran felt tears well in her eyes again as a bubble of hysteria built in her chest. 'At the moment I can think of about a million,' she said bitterly.

David could feel his frustration mounting. Mirry was sick and he needed to be with her. 'You know, Fran, I really don't need this now. My daughter is sick. At best she has a serious chest infection, at worst she could be rejecting her heart. I understand that you've been through worse than this. But I don't have time to play guessing games or outdo each other with who's suffered the most.'

Fran looked at David and knew he was right. He looked haggard and she saw lines on his face that she'd never noticed before. He didn't need her hysterics now but she still couldn't stay. She sat on the grass, plonking her bag beside her.

'What are the odds that she's in rejection?' she asked. She noticed the catch in her breath and how much even saying the word out loud hurt.

She felt him sit beside her and turned to face

him. His five o'clock shadow added to his look of profound tiredness.

'You heard Anne. Remote. But it is a possibility. I was worried about it before but I'm feeling much more positive now.'

'I guess it's always there, is it? At the back of your mind?'

He nodded. 'The sad fact is that most heart-transplant patients require more than one heart in their lifetime, particularly paediatric patients. Mirry and I were always going to have to face re-transplantation at some stage.'

Fran felt a roll of nausea spread through her. She hadn't known that. She felt her own heart, the one that David's love had helped glue back together, break all over again. Fran figured it was now totally beyond repair. 'So even if this is only a chest infection, Miranda will at some stage be looking at another transplant? Could possibly die while waiting for one?'

He nodded again, looking totally miserable, and she swore she saw the shine of tears glisten in his blue eyes.

Fran put her forehead against her bent knees, hugging them with her arms. 'I know you don't need this, David. But I can't do it. We already know I suck at supporting the men in my life. For God's sake, I pushed Jeremy into the arms of another woman because I failed to support him.'

Fran hadn't noticed that the stillness of the night was broken only by the constant hum of crickets and the occasional low purr of a car passing by until the silence from David stretched on and on. She watched without comment as he stood and paced back and forth in front of her.

He stopped in front of her and held out his hand. He pulled her up gently and dragged her into his arms, hugging her tight. They hugged for an eternity. Fran cried silent tears that soaked into David's shirt.

She pulled her head off his chest and looked up into his face. 'I hope you understand why this is too hard for me to stay and watch.'

Her face was tear-streaked again and even in the muted light he could see it was red and blotchy. 'I do,' he said quietly, 'I do understand.

I just don't want you to go. I'm sorry, I know that's not fair but I need you so much.'

'If this is rejection, I can't watch her die, David. It would be like Daisy all over again. I just can't. The first time around nearly killed me.'

Fran felt David stiffen a little in her arms and he pulled out of the embrace, letting his arms fall to his sides and taking a step back.

'It's not Daisy up there in that hospital bed, fighting for her life, Fran. It's Miranda. My child. Mine,' he said, pointing to his chest. 'And she needs you. I know this is hard for you but it's much, much worse for me. Daisy is dead and gone and there's nothing that you or I can do about that. But you can be there for Mirry. If you can't do it for me, at least do it for her.'

Fran felt a surge of emotion. Why had she ever let herself get involved? She should have known her happiness had been too good to be true. Now she was back in the awful emotional squall that had engulfed her two years ago. She'd put her heart on the line and it had been broken all over again.

She cleared her throat and waited for the emotion to clear because otherwise she knew she was going to battle to sound coherent. 'When I think about Miranda getting sick, and maybe dying, it gets me here.' She pounded her fist into her chest. 'I wish it didn't.' She sniffled and wiped the tears from her face. 'I'm just human, David, and all this is just too much for me to deal with.'

'There aren't any guarantees in life, Fran. Any of us could meet our maker at any time. Yes, Mirry has an increased risk but if you love her then the risk is worth it. Funny, I didn't peg you as a quitter,' he said quietly. 'Or someone who would turn their back on a sick girl.'

Fran felt like he was shooting bullets at her. 'It's not so black and white, David,' she said, her voice breaking.

'I love you, Fran. That's black and white. I want us to be together. That's black and white. The rest is up to you. I have to get back to Mirry. Are you coming with me?'

David held out his hand and held in his

breath. He had been tough, taken a gamble. Would it pay off?

Tears cascaded down her face as she shook her head at him and her shoulders shook with sobs as he handed her his car keys.

She pulled out the book from her bag that she thrown in earlier. 'Give this to Mirry for me. It was Daisy's favourite. Maybe you could read it to her.'

'Why don't you?' he said as he took the book.

Fran shook her head, tears shining in her eyes, before she turned on her heel and walked away.

'Drive carefully,' he whispered as he watched the woman he loved leave.

CHAPTER TEN

BEING BACK in the tunnel again was much worse than Fran had remembered. Even her short time in the light had dulled the unpleasant memories. The ache. The void. The ever-present sensation of claustrophobia. Not being able to breathe properly. Food stayed untouched in the fridge, washing piled up, brushing her teeth was a chore and washing her hair neglected.

She didn't go to work. Hell, she didn't even go out. She confined herself to the four walls and drew the wooden shutters. The only sunlight she saw was the occasional stray finger that managed to poke through the slats and even that hurt her eyes.

Fonzie followed her around the house with big worried eyes, only leaving her side to do his business. He snuggled into her wherever she prowled and often whimpered as he looked at her quizzically. Fran could see he was trying to be supportive but was going slowly stir crazy inside the house. Still, it wasn't enough impetus to spur her into the sunshine. Going out when she felt dead inside wasn't an option.

'Poor boy,' she whispered to him one day when he'd plonked his head in her lap. Fran was sitting curled up on the lounge chair, feigning interest in midday television. She scratched him in his sweet spot, just behind his ears. 'You miss your friends at the home, don't you? And Miranda.'

Fonzie lifted his head at her name and wagged his tail a couple of times. 'She's OK. She'll be home soon,' Fran told him, and Fonzie gave her face an enthusiastic lick.

David had called every day, usually twice. Fran had let the machine pick it up. The fact that it hadn't been rejection was an enormous relief, as was Mirry's fast response to the anti-biotics. David was hoping to be back at the weekend and every message ended the same. 'Mirry is asking for you.'

Fran's relief that her worst fears hadn't been realised had been short-lived. Mirry had escaped anything more serious this time. But there was always going to be a next time with Miranda. As David had said, sooner or later she was going to need another transplant and the thought that she could die while waiting was too painful for Fran to bear.

Glenda had rung every day, too. Fran had contacted her and organised some leave after she'd got back from Brisbane. Glenda had been surprised but hadn't pried and had been good enough to accommodate Fran's wishes. But Fran knew that she couldn't shirk her responsibilities for ever.

The question was, should she stay or should she go? Every part of her railed against moving again. She loved her little cliffside cottage and her job. She'd found happiness in this little community. But so much of it was linked to David and Miranda. Could she live next door and stay aloof? Separate from them? Out of their lives?

Miranda would be the hardest one to convince. Trying to keep a safe distance from her would be impossible. And as wrenching as it would be to remove herself from Miranda's orbit, staying and witnessing her inevitable declining health just wasn't something she could do.

Watching one girl she'd loved die had been the most gut-wrenching thing she had ever done. She knew she wasn't strong enough to go through the ups and downs of another.

By the end of the week Fran knew she had no choice. She couldn't stay. She rang the real-estate agent and they came straight away. Fran squinted as the harsh glare invaded the dark house when a youngish woman in a power suit came to the door. She came in and spoke contracts and the housing slump and about buyer's markets.

Fran didn't care. She didn't care if she sold at a loss. Money had never been an issue. All that mattered was that she moved on.

Where, she didn't know. Going back home for a start. Her parents, even Jeremy's mother, had worried endlessly about her in her six-month absence. It would be nice to see them again, and funnily enough the thought of returning didn't panic her as she'd thought it would. She'd done her running away and though she could never see herself living back in Canberra, going home for a while seemed the right thing to do.

Fran sat on the window-seat and watched with a heavy heart as the smart young woman hammered in a 'For Sale' sign on her footpath. Where was she going to find another such gem? A place by the beach where the waves provided the perfect white noise to lull her to sleep and the view from the window was all ocean and sand?

She wished she knew. But there was one thing she knew for sure—she was going to research the neighbours better next time. No children, no good-looking fathers and no transplant recipients. Surely that wasn't too much to ask?

* * *

The first thing David noticed when he pulled into his drive was the 'For Sale' sign.

'Why is Fran's house for sale, Daddy?'

Good question. 'I'm not sure, honey.'

Miranda started to cry. 'But I love Fran, Daddy. I thought you did, too. I want her to stay. I want you to marry her.'

'Mirry...' said David, looking at his devastated child. Poor Miranda had fretted for Fran and Fonzie all week and she'd chatted merrily all the way home in the car about heading straight for Fran's door the minute they got home. David hadn't known what their welcome was going to be like but he certainly hadn't expected this!

'Don't you love her, Daddy?' Miranda asked as she blew her runny nose on the tissue David gave her and dried her tears.

David looked at her earnest little face and realised this was going to be harder for her, for both of them, than he'd thought. All he could do was try and soften the blow and make Miranda see that Fran was complicated.

'Yes, darling, I do, but Fran has a lot on her

plate. You know about her daughter. I think being at the hospital with you brought back a lot of painful memories for her.'

'But we've made her happy, Daddy, haven't we?'

'Yes, sweetie, we have.' David smiled. But sometimes that just wasn't enough.

'Can I go and visit her, Daddy?'

David thought for a moment. He needed to talk to Fran first. 'Maybe tomorrow. You've had a tiring day and Dr Anne wants you to rest.'

'I've sat in a car for two hours, Daddy,' she groaned.

'Exactly—tiring stuff.' He winked. 'I want you to have a lie down.'

Miranda groaned louder. 'I've been lying down for a week!'

'You don't have to sleep.' He laughed. 'Just rest, OK? And tomorrow we'll go for a walk on the beach in the morning and go and visit Fran afterwards.'

Miranda weighed up the options. 'OK,' she grumbled good-naturedly.

* * *

David fussed over Miranda, settling her on the couch in front of the television. Despite her protestations that she wasn't tired, she promptly fell asleep. It was a good reminder of how sick she had been. Kids recovered fast and Mirry hadn't been any different, but the illness had taken its toll and her body was trying to tell her to rest even if her head totally rejected such a silly idea.

David took the opportunity to pop next door and see Fran. He had no idea if she'd let him in but he'd talk to her on the doorstep if he had to. He locked the door behind him, knowing that Mirry would be out of it for a good couple of hours and he didn't plan on staying too long next door.

The house looked totally shut up as he pushed open her gate, and he knew from Glenda that Fran hadn't been to work and no one had seen her around town. She'd gone all reclusive again. His heart pounded in his chest. He'd re-hearsed a thousand different things to say and he was no closer to deciding what to tell her.

He just wanted to see her. Look at her. He'd missed her like crazy all week despite her fleeing from his side. He knew he'd pushed her too far and he understood her reasons for leaving, he really did. But he needed to hold her again, very badly. Unfortunately the 'For Sale' sign told him he might not be welcome.

David took a deep breath and knocked on the door. He refused to believe that it was all over. He knew that a lot was riding on what he said when she opened the door.

Fonzie perked up his ears and barked excitedly at the knock. A visitor! He gave Fran an our-one-on-one-time's-been-great-but look and leapt off the bed where she'd been huddled all day.

She knew it was David. Could sense it. She almost didn't bother getting up but she knew she couldn't leave things the way they'd been in Brisbane and that she owed him at least a personal explanation as to why she was leaving.

She didn't stop and check her face in the mirror. Her hair hadn't been washed in days, and she didn't bother to get out of her oversized

T-shirt to answer the door. Her appearance had ranked fairly low on the important scale recently and it might help to soften the blow if she looked like something he wouldn't want to touch with a ten-foot bargepole!

David's eyes devoured her as she opened the door and winced and blinked at the bright light. Her bedroom was quite dark with the shutters closed and the tunnel-like gloom within the house suited her mood perfectly.

'Come in,' she said, eager to shut the door and bar the light.

David followed her inside, noticing the weight she'd lost despite the shapeless T-shirt and the defeated set to her shoulders.

'Coffee?' she asked, flicking on the jug in the kitchen.

He shook his head. 'No. I can't stay. Mirry is sleeping. I don't want her to wake up and wonder where I am.'

Fran nodded and turned back to make herself one and to remove him from her line of vision. She hadn't seen him for a week and the fact that she loved him hadn't changed. No amount of reasoning about the wise thing to do mattered when confronted by the man she loved. Seeing him again after a week's absence was torture and she just wanted to go throw herself at him and feel his arms around her. She felt like she was barely keeping it all together.

'Thank you for keeping me updated on Miranda's condition,' she said stiffly.

'You didn't return my calls.' David sat at the breakfast bar and watched her.

Fran stirred her coffee, not missing the gentle tone of accusation in his voice. She tapped the teaspoon on the side of the mug and placed it in the sink. 'I'm leaving, David. What would have been the point? Better to make a clean break.'

'So you're running away.'

'Yes,' she admitted quietly.

'Why? I know you love me, Fran. Love us. It doesn't make any sense.'

Her eyes welled with tears and she felt a sob rise in her throat. 'Because if I love you this much now, how bad is going to be in a year, or two or five?' She knew her voice was rising and that soon she wouldn't be able to speak as her voice would be completely broken with pent up emotions. 'How much harder is it going to be to watch Mirry go through another transplant? What if I can't do it then? If it's too confronting? What if I'm useless to you?' She sat at the breakfast bar with him and put a hand on his arm. 'It's better to get out now while I still have a chance to recover.'

'It doesn't matter where you run, Fran, It's too late. We're in your heart, in your soul. You can run but we'll always be with you.'

'It won't be the same as being right here. Living next door. Having you both as a constant reminder.'

'Where will you go?'

'Home…for a while. Then I don't know. Start over somewhere else.'

'So that's how it's going to be, then, is it? The minute an emotional entanglement comes along, you're just going to skip town and start somewhere new? Just never get involved ever? Ever?'

Fran felt a tear roll down her cheek at the lonely picture he painted. She shrugged. 'It can be done. I shouldn't have let you two in. I was doing OK.'

'No, Fran. You weren't. You were existing but that was about it.' David's voice was gentle to soften the harsh reality and he watched her as she got up and walked back over to the sink.

'You're wrong,' she said, staring out at the sea view. 'Compared to the previous two years I was practically fully functioning. I'd already made a decision about reclaiming my life. You guys just hastened the process. I would have got there…eventually. I'll be OK by myself. In fact, I think I prefer it.'

Fran swallowed the lie and felt dead inside. Before coming to Ashworth Bay, having another relationship, falling in love again hadn't been on her agenda. But now that it had happened, the thought of going back to the deep despair of isolation was heart-breaking.

'I don't believe you,' he said, and reached down and patted a forlorn-looking Fonzie who had plonked himself at David's feet. 'You may have thought you wanted to be alone, but what about Fonzie? Why did you get him? Because you were lonely and needed company. You're human, Fran, we all need that.'

Fran gripped the sink at the accuracy of David's words. How had he got to know her in such a short period of time? 'Fonzie was part of me reclaiming my life,' she said, and turned back to face him. Her heart squeezed painfully in her chest. She loved him so much and if he didn't go soon she'd do something really stupid, like ask him to hold her.

'Look, I'm leaving on Monday. There's nothing you can say that will change my mind. I'm sorry things got messy and that Mirry got caught up in it. Just go, OK?'

David looked down at Fonzie who seemed to be pleading with him to make Fran see sense. *Don't look at me, buddy, I'm all out of ideas. Except for maybe one.* 'Can I bring Miranda over tomorrow to say goodbye?'

Fran felt the impact of the idea slam into her. No! 'I don't think that's a good idea,' she said.

'She saw the 'For Sale' sign. She's heart-broken, Fran. You can't just walk away without saying goodbye.'

Fran bit her tongue to stop the rush of tears. She knew he was right. She had to try and soften the blow for Mirry as much as she could. 'OK…sure.'

David nodded. 'Thank you.'

Fran nodded back. They stood staring at each other for a few moments. Fran held on to the sink behind her because she knew if she wasn't anchored to something, she was going to run to him and never let him go.

David clenched and unclenched his fists, wanting to go to her as well, but didn't think he could keep facing her rejection. He didn't want to force Fran or have to talk her into anything. He wanted her to come to him of her own free accord. To say she knew that what lay ahead could be painful but life without him would be more painful.

He looked at her utter dejection. 'Oh, Fran,' he whispered.

She shook her head vigorously and turned back to the sink because she knew he was going to come closer and she didn't have the power to stop him. She emptied her mostly full cup of coffee down the sink. 'Just go. Please,' she pleaded, 'just go.'

David, who had drawn closer and was about to put his hands on her shoulders, paused and took a step back. The complexity of her issues seemed overwhelming suddenly and he doubted whether his touch would cut it. For the first time since Mirry had got sick he really believed it was over.

'I'll see you tomorrow with Mirry.'

She nodded and he wondered as he turned to go if it was actually physically painful for her to be holding herself so erect.

Fran was as prepared as she was ever going to be when the doorbell chimed. Fonzie barked enthusiastically and she could hear Mirry's excited chatter as she approached the door.

She had made an effort with her appearance. Washed her hair and put something on that fitted. She didn't want Mirry's last memory of her to be the same as her first. And there was nothing wrong with a little bit of dressing the part. If she looked together then hopefully she could actually pull it off.

But when she opened the door to them she knew she was going to fail—badly. Standing before her were two people she loved with every fibre of her being. David looked tall and handsome and resigned and Miranda looked her usual energetic self, jiggling on the spot. Saying goodbye was going to be impossible.

'Fran!' exclaimed Mirry, and threw herself at Fran's body, her skinny arms easily circling Fran's waist.

'Hey, you,' said Fran, ejecting the tremble from her voice. She looked into Miranda's beautiful face, framed by those disobedient red curls. Miranda grabbed her enthusiastically and pulled Fran towards her, giving her another big hug. 'I missed you, Fran.'

Fran heard the steady beating of Miranda's heart. 'You look great. Much better than the last time I saw you!'

Mirry nodded at her and wriggled out of Fran's hold to get to Fonzie, who was squirming impatiently for a bit of loving from Miranda. David stepped into the house and they watched Miranda and Fonzie get reacquainted.

David watched Fran surreptitiously. Her face was a mixture of emotions. Joy and pain, happiness and sorrow. How could she walk away from them?

She had to. She felt her heart swelling and swelling as her love for Miranda and David grew with each second they were in her house, but she knew how bad it felt to lose that. Better to let it go now when their acquaintance had been short and the feelings weren't as deep.

Miranda stopped playing with Fonzie and approached Fran.

'Daddy says that being at the hospital with me freaked you out. If I promise to never get sick again, will you stay? If you stay, Daddy and I will make you happy for ever. Please, stay, Fran. We love you. And Fonzie.'

Fonzie wagged his tail. Fran blinked at

Miranda's candour and felt her heart break. She could do this. She had said goodbye to two people she had loved before and she could do it again.

'I love you, too, sweetie. I really do, but it's time to move on for me. I know it's hard to understand, but I hope you will one day. Anyway, I'll write and I may even come back for a visit.'

Miranda's face crumbled and Fran scooped the girl into her arms again. She refused to shed any tears as Mirry unloaded hers. If she started she wouldn't stop and she had to be the adult here.

She glanced up at David who also looked like his heart was being torn out. He probably hated her right now. His job as a father was to protect his child from hurt and there was nothing he could do to fix this.

'Anyway,' said Fran, extricating herself from Miranda's vice-like grip, 'I thought, if it was OK with your father, you might like to keep Fonzie for me. He needs someone energetic and he'd miss everyone at the home too much and I'm not sure where I'll be for a while...'

Miranda's face lit up like a New Year's Eve firework display. 'Do you mean it, Fran? Really?' She turned to her father. 'Can I, Daddy, oh, please, can I?'

Fran tried to sell the idea further. 'I'm sorry, I should have asked first. I know there are pet issues with transplant patients but he's fully vaccinated and she's really very good at washing her hands.'

David looked at Fran and realised the sacrifice she was making. Fonzie had symbolised the start of a new life and the determination to drag herself out of the abyss she'd been languishing in. Fran loved that dog. But she loved Mirry more and knew that it was in the best interests of both of them.

Fran was relieved to see the suggestion had worked. Miranda had cheered up and she hoped that having Fonzie would soften the blow of her leaving. Losing Fonzie as well as David and Miranda would be hard, she knew that, but Fonzie loved it here, too, and Fran knew this was a win-win situation.

David searched Fran's eyes, wanting to make sure she meant it. She nodded at him.

'Of course, darling,' he said, and Miranda cheered as she waltzed around the room with Fonzie in her arms.

Fran looked at her watch, suddenly overwhelmed again by what she was giving up. Now it was done she just wanted them to go. 'Well.' She cleared her voice of its huskiness. 'I have to go and see Glenda.'

David knew they were being summarily dismissed but could sense how precariously she was hanging on. He groped around, desperately trying to find the key. The right words that would make her see sense and stay.

'Please, Fran,' he said huskily, 'if you won't stay for you, then stay for me. I don't want to go through this alone any more. I don't think I'm strong enough to watch Mirry go through another op. The tests and biopsies are hard enough. I don't want to do it by myself any more. I can't. I need someone to lean on.'

'Yes, you can, David,' she said, her voice

strong. 'You can and you will because she's your daughter, and while there is still breath left in you, you will do what needs to be done for her. Because that's what parents do. David…do whatever it takes because nothing is more precious.'

'Fran,' he whispered, and he didn't have to fake the mournful, desperate edge.

He held his arms out to her but she stepped away from him. If she let him touch her now, hold her, she'd never be strong enough to do what she had to do.

'Goodbye,' she said, proud of the sliver of steel in her voice.

All three of them looked at her. Fonzie flopped his head from side to side, staring at her with big brown eyes. Miranda looked ready to cry again. David opened his mouth to say something.

'I'm going to be fine,' she said, emotion making her voice husky. To prove it, she gave Fonzie an ear scratch, Miranda a tight squeeze and David a quick peck on the cheek. 'I'll call, I promise.'

Defeated, David rounded up Miranda and Fonzie and moved them out. Fran watched from the doorstep, determined to put on a brave face until the end. She waved at them as they left, walking side by side to the gate.

This was for the best. This was for the best. Please, don't look back. Just keep walking. She could do this. Their acquaintance had been brief. The pain would go. She'd had worse. She felt the tunnel encroaching around her and sucking her back in, and the despair bubble up into her chest.

And then all three turned in unison and looked back at her, their love shining in their eyes, and she knew she couldn't do it. She couldn't go back into the tunnel when she'd fought so long and hard to get free of it. And she couldn't let the three things that had come to mean so much to her in the last months walk out of her life. Not when she loved them more than her own life.

What the hell had she been thinking? Did she really think how long you knew someone was directly proportional to your strength of feeling for them? That knowing someone for months made it easier to say goodbye than if you'd known them for years? Loving someone for a minute or a lifetime didn't matter. It only mattered that you loved them.

'Wait.' The command was wrenched from deep inside her.

'Fran?' David saw the conflict on Fran's face and held his breath.

She ran down the path and stood in front of him. 'I was wrong. Please, don't go. I love you. I want to be with you.' Fonzie licked her leg and she looked down at him and Miranda. 'All of you.'

Mirry squealed and launched herself at Fran, jumping up and down as she hugged her.

'Really?' asked David, not daring to hope.

'Really.' She nodded and smiled.

He opened his arms to her and she sank into them gratefully, bursting into tears. Mirry's arms snaked around both of them and David kissed Fran's hair until she quietened.

Fonzie jumped up, wanting some of the

action, and Miranda broke away, chasing him round and round the yard in her excitement.

David gave Fran a brief passionate kiss that held so much promise. 'Are you sure about this?' he said, wiping her tears away with his fingers.

'Yes.' She nodded. 'I can't promise that it's all going to be plain sailing but I love you and I don't want to live another day without you. I can't believe I almost let you walk away.'

Fran kissed him and he believed her. But there was some unfinished stuff between them. 'What happens if Miranda gets sick again?'

Fran pulled back a little. She supposed it was a fair enough question. 'Look, I know that there's a lot of potential pain for me in this relationship, David. If things go bad with Mirry, that will be really hard for me. But it'll be even harder for you. You're going to need my support and I want to be there for you. I'm sorry I deserted you last week. It really threw me for a loop but I'm going into this with my eyes open now and I can promise to be stronger and better next time round. Whatever our future holds, I need you to know that I'd rather have an eternity of pain than miss out on another day of loving you.'

'Good answer.' David smiled down into her tear-stained face. Her words were like music to his ears. Fran wasn't totally healed and perhaps part of her would always be a little broken, but she wanted them. Loved them. And that was enough for him.

Miranda and Fonzie stopped what they were doing and watched the two adults embracing. They looked at each other, chocolate brown eyes meeting sea green.

Life had been pretty damn good before.

But now...now it was perfect.

MEDICAL ROMANCE™

Large Print

Titles for the next six months…

April

RESCUE AT CRADLE LAKE	Marion Lennox
A NIGHT TO REMEMBER	Jennifer Taylor
THE DOCTORS' NEW-FOUND FAMILY	Laura MacDonald
HER VERY SPECIAL CONSULTANT	Joanna Neil
A SURGEON, A MIDWIFE: A FAMILY	Gill Sanderson
THE ITALIAN DOCTOR'S BRIDE	Margaret McDonagh

May

THE CHRISTMAS MARRIAGE RESCUE	Sarah Morgan
THEIR CHRISTMAS DREAM COME TRUE	Kate Hardy
A MOTHER IN THE MAKING	Emily Forbes
THE DOCTOR'S CHRISTMAS PROPOSAL	Laura Iding
HER MIRACLE BABY	Fiona Lowe
THE DOCTOR'S LONGED-FOR BRIDE	Judy Campbell

June

THE MIDWIFE'S CHRISTMAS MIRACLE	Sarah Morgan
ONE NIGHT TO WED	Alison Roberts
A VERY SPECIAL PROPOSAL	Josie Metcalfe
THE SURGEON'S MEANT-TO-BE BRIDE	Amy Andrews
A FATHER BY CHRISTMAS	Meredith Webber
A MOTHER FOR HIS BABY	Leah Martyn

MILLS & BOON®

Live the emotion

0307 LP 2P P1 Medical

MEDICAL ROMANCE™

Large Print

July

THE SURGEON'S MIRACLE BABY — Carol Marinelli
A CONSULTANT CLAIMS HIS BRIDE — Maggie Kingsley
THE WOMAN HE'S BEEN WAITING FOR
— Jennifer Taylor
THE VILLAGE DOCTOR'S MARRIAGE — Abigail Gordon
IN HER BOSS'S SPECIAL CARE — Melanie Milburne
THE SURGEON'S COURAGEOUS BRIDE — Lucy Clark

August

A WIFE AND CHILD TO CHERISH — Caroline Anderson
THE SURGEON'S FAMILY MIRACLE — Marion Lennox
A FAMILY TO COME HOME TO — Josie Metcalfe
THE LONDON CONSULTANT'S RESCUE — Joanna Neil
THE DOCTOR'S BABY SURPRISE — Gill Sanderson
THE SPANISH DOCTOR'S CONVENIENT BRIDE
— Meredith Webber

September

A FATHER BEYOND COMPARE — Alison Roberts
AN UNEXPECTED PROPOSAL — Amy Andrews
SHEIKH SURGEON, SURPRISE BRIDE — Josie Metcalfe
THE SURGEON'S CHOSEN WIFE — Fiona Lowe
A DOCTOR WORTH WAITING FOR — Margaret McDonagh
HER L.A. KNIGHT — Lynne Marshall

MILLS & BOON®
Live the emotion

0307 LP 2P P2 Medical